THE BILLIONAIRE'S OBESSION

Blake

J. S. SCOTT

Billionaire Unknown

Cover by Wax Creative

ISBN: 978-1-939962-98-0 (Print)
ISBN: 978-1-939962-67-6 (E-Book)

Contents

Prologue

Blake

Christmas Eve, Twelve Years Ago

What in the hell was I doing?

Basically, I was freezing my ass off looking for a runaway girl in the middle of a snowstorm on Christmas Eve. What really pissed me off was the fact that she was a spoiled eighteen-year-old female who I'd never liked in the first place.

My nickname for her when were kids had been Cruella de Vil for as long as I could remember, and I referred to her by that name so often that I almost failed to remember that her real name was Harper Lawson. She was the second youngest member of the Lawson family, friends of the Colter family for as long as I could remember.

That's why I'm out here freezing my balls off on Christmas Eve.

There was very little I *wouldn't* do for my mother. But right at the moment, I wished I didn't love her quite so much. I never had been able to tolerate seeing my mother upset. And, since the spoiled brat's mother was best friends with mine, of course Mom was worried.

Call me an idiot, but I volunteered for this torture just so I didn't have to see the stress on my mom's face.

I hadn't seen Harper Lawson in years, even though she lived in another small town fairly close to where we did in Rocky Springs, Colorado. I was on college break, and Harper had just graduated from high school. Thankfully, Mom had stopped trying to push a friendship between me and the younger Lawson girls when I was still in grade school, when I finally told her how much I disliked Harper because she was downright mean. Her younger sister, Danica, was a heck of a lot nicer, but I hadn't seen much of her, either. I had run into the Lawson brothers occasionally, but because we went to different schools, we barely knew any of them.

Only Harper had ever irritated the hell out of me. She'd always gone out of her way to be a child dictator, and she flaunted her parents' wealth like it made her better than anyone else. It hadn't mattered that the Colters were wealthy, too. She'd been equal opportunity nasty to every person she came into contact with when she was a kid.

Judging by my current frigid trek through the snow, she hadn't changed one damn bit.

I smirked as my rubber boots plowed through the deep snowdrifts on the sidewalk, finding it hard to believe that Harper might actually be in the Denver homeless shelter I was looking for during one of the nastiest blizzards we'd seen in a long time.

Apparently, she'd run away after her parents had finally set their foot down on her endless spending of money she hadn't earned. They'd taken away her credit cards, her brand-new car she'd gotten for graduation, and most of her extravagant purchases because she had no desire to go to college. Obviously, she figured that since her parents were rich, she didn't need an education. Her plans were probably focused on becoming a rich socialite for life.

Fuck! I hated rich kids with that attitude. I busted my ass in college, and not a single Colter child had ever felt entitled. We were all either working on our careers, or planning our own futures. We had a lot of money, but not a single one of us ever considered just being idle.

I'd heard the Lawson brothers were all going to college. But Harper apparently didn't want to work that hard.

Really, I was kind of surprised that her parents had never recognized how self-centered their daughter was before now.

Once the Lawsons had realized how incredibly spoiled Harper was, and that she'd never planned to get any higher education, they'd finally decided to cut her off. Harper had immediately balked and run away from home. Well, technically, she *wasn't* a runaway. She was eighteen, so she wasn't a juvenile. But she sure as hell acted like one.

Who in the hell ran away just because mommy and daddy took away her car and her credit cards?

"She's still a spoiled brat," I muttered irritably as I kept walking through the drifting snow, the cold starting to whip right through my winter jacket and jeans. "If Mom hadn't been so freaked out, I would have stayed warm and comfortable at home, celebrating Christmas with my own family instead of worrying about somebody else's problems."

Unfortunately, Aileen Colter worried about everybody. My mother was one of the most caring people I knew, and the glue that held our family together after my father had died years ago. She was such good friends with Harper's mother that she was horrified at the thought of a young woman lost somewhere in a blizzard by herself.

I was a sucker. The sad look on my mother's face had prompted me to jump into a helicopter from Rocky Springs to Denver with a storm coming in, just to find some obnoxious chick who couldn't function without her luxury vehicle and credit cards.

I finally located the makeshift shelter, grateful for the warmth once I stepped inside.

There were bodies everywhere, most of them on sleeping mats with a blanket on the floor. Because of the weather, I knew most of the shelters were overloaded.

I scanned the people on the floor, some of them sleeping, but many sitting up with a blanket around their body.

My heart sank as I saw the people in tattered clothing, and inhaled the stench of unwashed bodies.

Was this the best they could expect on Christmas Eve? Just stepping into the place reminded me of how damn lucky I'd been. The Colters were ungodly wealthy, and because my father had already passed away, that wealth had been distributed to all of his kids and my mother.

At the ripe old age of twenty-two, I was already rich, but I'd never for a moment *not* considered working, or getting a college degree. My dad had been an educated man, and I knew he'd wanted the same for all his children. My identical twin brother, Marcus, had taken over my father's legacy, while the rest of us were busy planning our destinies by continuing on to college. Marcus had it the worst, trying to go to school and keep up with what was happening with our dad's international business interests. I knew as soon as my twin graduated, he'd be traveling the world.

And damn…I was going to miss him.

"Can I help you? I'm afraid we don't have any space left." The female voice was low and compassionate.

The middle-aged woman smiled at me, a sympathetic smile that I didn't deserve.

"No, ma'am," I answered reassuringly, wanting her to know she didn't have to put me up for the night. "I'm looking for someone. I don't need to take up one of your beds."

Fumbling in my coat pocket, I drew out the latest picture of Harper, her graduation photo. "Have you seen her?"

The lady took the picture and examined it closely. "Looks a little familiar. But I can't quite place her. We've taken in a lot of young people."

I took the photo and put it back in my pocket. "Mind if I look around a little?" *Jesus!* I hoped the tip that had come in about Harper being in this place hadn't been wrong.

The overworked woman shrugged. "Feel free to search for your friend. I'd like to see one less person be alone on Christmas."

I nodded, and then made my way around the large room, my eyes scanning all of the desperate faces occupying the space. Finally, I did a double-take on one solitary female, almost discarding the notion that I might be looking at Harper.

The young woman had the same blonde hair, and was probably about the same age. But everything else about her was…wrong. I edged closer to her and her position sitting across the room against the concrete wall, her arms wrapped around her body like she was cold.

As I approached, I could tell she'd been crying. "Harper?" I said her name in a loud voice from several feet away, and she immediately turned her head to look up at me.

She frowned and swiped away the remnants of her tears as she answered, "Colter?"

I nodded, unable to look away from the tortured look in her dark-green eyes and the despair I saw there.

Christ! It *was* really Harper, but she looked nothing like her sophisticated picture. She was in a pair of ratty jeans and a sweater rather than designer clothing. She was wearing no jewelry, not even the diamond pendant or the rings I knew her parents hadn't taken away. And her angelic face was completely devoid of makeup. Her blonde hair hung down to her shoulders with a natural curl that was far more attractive than the upswept, sophisticated style in her picture.

I crouched next to her. "I'm here to take you home. Your family has been worried sick."

She shook her head. "I can't go back there."

"You can," I said firmly. "Problem is, we may have to stay in Denver tonight. I'm not sure we can get back to Rocky Springs in this weather. But at least we can vacate this bed so somebody else can use it."

She slowly nodded, and then rose to her feet. "That would be good. So many people are in need of a warm place to be right now. I'll go with you."

I took her hand simply because she looked so damn lost, and led her toward the door of the shelter, giving the woman running it a large donation before I hauled Harper out the door after she retrieved a jacket that wasn't going to be nearly warm enough for the current weather.

Guiding her a few blocks away to the hotel room my brother Marcus had been able to procure before I'd started searching for Harper, I suddenly remembered it had been the only available room in Denver. Because of the snowstorm and the holidays, everything had been booked solid.

Once we entered the room of the somewhat rundown hotel, I informed her, "We'll have to share. This was the only available room we could find."

She shrugged. "It doesn't matter."

"Harper, everything will be okay. As soon as the helicopter can fly, we'll get you back home." I didn't like her, but her downtrodden mood was making me feel a little sorry for her.

"Mom, Dad, and my older brothers will give me hell," she stated flatly. "They wanted me to go."

Even though the room was warm enough, she shuddered.

I started making a pot of coffee as I answered, "They didn't want you to go. They wanted you to grow up."

The coffeemaker sputtered for a moment before it started to brew. There wasn't a ton of stuff in the small space. A small TV and the coffee stuff was sitting on a cheap brown console, and there was a king-sized bed with the most god-awful, gaudy bedspread I'd ever seen. Other than two small bedside tables, there was no other furniture in the room except for a tiny, rickety-looking table with two very worn wooden chairs.

I was slightly worried about checking out the bathroom. I'd checked in and dropped my duffel bag, and then headed out almost immediately to look for Harper. I took a cautious glance around the corner. It was no fancy hotel bathroom, but it had a shower and a toilet, and I was relieved when I noticed that it looked fairly clean.

I poured out the coffee when it was done, handing Harper one of the mugs. "Here. I don't know what you want in it."

"Thanks," she answered quietly, and then proceeded to drink it black as she seated herself at the small table. "How did you get roped into finding me? I almost didn't recognize you. I haven't seen you since we were kids."

I sat across from her, sat my mug on the table, and then shrugged out of my jacket and swept the hat from my head. "Almost everybody in town was looking for you. Your parents were afraid you'd been kidnapped or lost in the storm."

"I'm surprised they cared," she answered morosely.

I opened my mouth to ask her if she thought they'd stop caring just because they took away her credit cards, and give her a lecture about being a spoiled brat. I closed it again when I saw tears leaking from her beautiful, emerald-green eyes.

"They care," I answered simply, suddenly wanting to comfort her, which was highly unusual for me when it came to Harper. Mostly…I wanted to avoid her.

"I think I understand that now. Honestly, after seeing how badly other people are suffering, I feel like a major bitch for leaving my warm, comfortable home," she admitted openly. "I deserved everything my parents and brothers said to me."

"Have you been at the shelter the whole time?" I knew she'd been missing for several days.

"Yes. I took buses to Denver, but I only had a small amount of cash. Then the storm hit, and I had nowhere to go."

The sadness in her voice made my heart clench. "Your mom said you'd still have your jewelry on. And you were last seen wearing a designer pants suit."

"I gave my jewelry to a family who got turned away," she confessed in a husky whisper. "They had nothing, and they needed a place to stay. The little one was cold, so I gave her my blanket."

It was the last thing I expected Harper to tell me, and I gaped at her in astonishment. Recovering quickly, I asked, "And your clothing?"

"Silk," she answered in disgust. "I was so cold that I went through the donations at the shelter and found something warmer to wear."

I frowned. "Harper, are you okay?"

She looked up at me and slowly shook her head. "I've never seen how many homeless people there are, so many families that can't even manage to keep their homes. I've never even been to this part of Denver. It's so…sad."

"So you gave away everything you had to help a big family survive? You could have pawned the jewelry yourself," I suggested, surprised she hadn't done just that.

"I couldn't. They were gifts from my parents. So I decided to stay here until I could figure something out. But when I met that family, and they were so desperate, I couldn't let them walk away into the cold again. I'm hoping they found a room."

She sounded so disheartened that I quickly replied, "I'm sure they did. Things just started to get completely full up last night."

I didn't really know that for sure, but how in the hell could I let her worry about whether or not her sacrifice had helped the family find a place? Judging by what her mother had told me about Harper's jewelry, it would have fetched enough money for their needs for quite some time.

I could still hardly believe that Harper, the selfish, mean, spoiled child I'd once been forced to socialize with as a kid was the same person I was looking at now.

She sighed as she cradled her coffee mug. "I hope they're okay."

"You're different," I blurted out, without censoring my words.

Harper shot me a sad smile right before she took a sip of her coffee, then set it back down on the table. "Maybe I grew up. Right now I hate myself."

"Why?"

"Because before I landed in that shelter, I never bothered to look around and see the rest of the people around me. I grew up in a privileged world, and I stayed there. I think my parents did me a favor. When I see all of the people who actually care about homeless families, and the others who have fallen on hard times, I realize what a bitch I've always been."

Her candid explanation and self-deprecation affected me in a way that made my heart bleed for the way she'd suddenly been thrust into reality. Sure, maybe she had needed to grow up. But she was only eighteen, and after being sheltered by her parents for so long, the desperation she'd been witness to had to be sobering and traumatic.

In some ways, it was her parents' fault, too. My dad had died years ago, but my mom always kept us Colters very aware of our obligation to give a damn about those less fortunate than we were. It was ingrained in every Colter from the time we were young.

We'd volunteered in soup kitchens.

All of us had plenty of charities we supported with enthusiasm.

We donated Christmas toys.

And none of us were ever unaware of the suffering in the world.

What in the hell had Harper's parents been thinking? Sure, they were wealthy, but sheltering their kids from the rougher parts of life hadn't done Harper any favors.

"If you realize what you did was wrong, you're not a bitch," I assured her in a husky voice. Really, I admired the fact that she'd opened her eyes and heart to those people in need.

I was also shocked as shit that she'd cared.

I hadn't seen Harper since we were young, but she'd grown into a beautiful young woman, and she was so much more attractive when she was real—just like this.

"Thanks," she said in a thoughtful voice. "But I don't think I deserve your effort to make me feel better about myself."

As I slugged down my coffee, I pretty much thought what she really needed was cheering up. She looked pretty damned shell-shocked and depressed.

"I need to call your folks. Do you want to talk to them?"

A panicked looked flared in her eyes. "Not yet. Please. I know I have to face them and fess up to what I've done. But I just need a little time."

I nodded, understanding her confusion. "No problem. I'll let them know you're safe and I'll get you home as soon as I can."

I stood and pulled my phone out of my pocket and made some calls.

Later That Night…

I laid in bed with Harper, wondering if she was sleeping. Throughout the evening, it had gotten harder and harder to ignore my attraction to the new and improved woman I'd gotten to know this evening.

Since it was Christmas Eve, I'd finagled her into going out to a local pub, one of the few that were open, and just hanging out with me after we'd had dinner there. She'd told me more about her experience with the homeless, and how scared she was when she'd found herself on her own with nothing but the shelter to keep her warm and safe.

In turn, I found myself talking a lot about my past, sharing things with her that I hadn't opened up about for a long time.

I had no doubt—Harper *had* changed. I'd told her parents what I thought over the phone, and they'd blamed themselves for some of the problems between them and their daughter. I'd also called my own mother just to tell her I loved her, and I hoped I'd be back home with the family tomorrow.

Honestly, I'd enjoyed my time with Harper so much this evening that I really didn't care when I made it back home. All my siblings would be around until after New Year's, and I found myself wanting to be in Harper's company more than I should.

Every moment, every second of the time I'd spent with her, my dick had been as hard as a rock, refusing to ignore the combustible chemistry that was starting to explode between me and Harper. The pull kept getting stronger and stronger. By the time I saw her wearing one of the extra T-shirts I brought with me to Denver, I nearly lost it.

She'd needed something to sleep in.

I'd given her my T-shirt.

That was a fucking mistake.

Too much skin.

Too many fantasies.

Too many times I'd laid here and thought about those shapely bare legs wrapped around my waist as she shuddered in climax.

I needed to fuck Harper something fierce, but I was determined to ignore it. However, my brain was refusing to let the attraction go, and my cock was a total fail. I was as hard as a rock, even though her naked limbs were now covered with blankets. But holy hell, I could still picture them in my mind. *Was she thinking about me at all?* For all I knew, she was sleeping.

"Are you awake?" she whispered softly.

Ignore it, Colter. Don't answer. Act like you're sleeping.

"Yeah," I answered recklessly.

"Can I move closer to you?" she asked in a pleading voice.

She was still scared, and still stuck in Denver. She was vulnerable, and I knew I should just be here to talk to her. But something inside me wouldn't let it end there.

"Come here," I requested firmly, opening my arms so I could hold her.

She scooted closer, and to my surprise, she swung one leg over my hips and clung to me like I was her shelter in the storm. Her head rested on my chest, and her arms wrapped around my shoulders, her body plastered full-length down my side.

Her leg was just north of one very hard dick, and as I wrapped my arms around her shivering body, all I fucking wanted was to make her happy again.

Well…I wanted to fuck her, too. But my instinct to protect her was just as strong.

"Thank you," she said in a low, contented purr. "You're so warm."

No doubt I was blazing hot. I could feel her nipples through the thin cotton of my T-shirt, and that leg over my hips was fueling horny fantasies that I couldn't control.

"Better?" I asked, my voice cracking with desire.

"Much," she said in a blissful voice as she squirmed against me.

"Don't move!" My voice was harsh, and I hated myself for that.

She lifted her head. "What's wrong?"

Was it possible that Harper could possibly be *that* naïve? I was honest with her. "I want to be here with you. I want to hold you. But Jesus Christ! I want to fuck you so bad that I can hardly control myself. If you start squirming around, I'm afraid I'll lose it. You're a beautiful woman, Harper."

"I'm attracted to you, too," she admitted in a hushed whisper.

She spoke like she was just recognizing her desire, and her innocence made me half crazy. "Have you been with a guy?"

"Dates. Kissing. Never much beyond that."

"Why?"

"I never had this weird fluttering in my stomach like I have with you. I've never wanted anything more with any of the guys I've dated."

I swallowed hard as I realized she was a virgin.

Mine!

I wanted this woman to belong to me in a way she never had with any other male before.

"Wait until you find the right man," I advised, wanting desperately to tell her I *was* that right guy.

But more than likely, it was just hormones. I was twenty-two years old, and I wanted to get laid as frequently as possible. It had been months. I didn't have a regular girlfriend, but there was plenty of fucking around on campus. Lately, I'd been busy studying for finals. Maybe my dick was just complaining because I wasn't using it much these days.

Harper hesitantly threaded her hands into my hair and stretched up to lay one very sweet kiss on my mouth. "That's just it. This is the only time I've ever felt like this. I want you."

I rolled her under me in one swift movement. "For God's sake, don't say that," I rumbled, my heart hammering as I felt her soft curves beneath me. "My control isn't good right now, Harper."

That was an understatement. I was actually breathing so hard that my chest hurt.

"Then let go of your control. I'm eighteen. I want to see what it feels like to be with a man," she cajoled, spearing her fingers into my hair again and urging my head down.

Just like that…I lost it.

I could see her face in the dim, moonlit room, and I zoomed in on her lips, swooping to devour her like I'd wanted to do all evening.

I kissed her like I needed to do it to keep on living, and that was exactly how I felt.

Harper seemed to melt into me, moaning softly against my lips, a sound of pleasure that just made me more desperate to be the first guy—the only man—to possess her.

I came up from the passionate, carnal embrace with my arms bracing my weight, panting like an overheated dog. *Jesus! What the hell was happening to me?*

"I. Can't. Fucking. Do. This!" Every word was painful for me, tearing my guts apart.

"What? Why?" Harper sounded confused.

She also sounded aroused as hell, which was pretty much killing me.

"You're a virgin. I can't do this."

"I'm a virgin because I've never wanted to be with a guy. It's not like I was saving myself for marriage. It's just...no guy has ever turned me on enough to want it."

I groaned. "Don't tell me that."

"It's true," she argued. "Please. Keep making me feel good. I like it."

I wanted her to feel so fucking good that she'd be ruined for any other guy. Forever!

I rolled to her side and slowly ran my hand up her thigh, strangling back a feral sound as I reached her delicate, silken panties that were soaked with her juices. "You're so wet."

"I ache," Harper whimpered softly.

"I know, baby. It's okay." I slid my finger under the elastic and stroked a finger through her slit. Her silken heat drove me nearly insane. "I'll make the ache go away," I promised as I slid her panties off her body, tossing them to the side of the bed.

"Promise?" she asked hesitantly.

I sat up and gripped the bottom of my T-shirt. "I promise. But I need you naked."

She lifted her arms in an action of trust, allowing me to peel the shirt from her body. Once it had joined her discarded underwear, I just gaped at her in the moonlight.

Her soft curves and generous breasts made my mouth go dry, and my cock strain against the zipper of my jeans. My upper body was bare, but I'd worn my jeans to bed so I didn't freak her out.

"Aren't you getting naked, too?" she asked inquisitively.

Oh, hell no. Not right now. I'd be inside her in a heartbeat. "Not yet."

"Then what are you doing?"

"Looking at you," I answered honestly. "I've never wanted a woman this way before. It's kind of a first for me, too."

"You're not a virgin," she argued.

"I'm definitely not," I agreed with a grin. "But you're...different, Harper."

"Because I've never been with a guy before?"

I shook my head. "No. Because you're you."

I couldn't explain how I felt. Hell, I didn't understand it myself.

My hands were a little shaky as I cupped her breasts, teasing both nipples with my thumbs. They were already hard, but they peaked up even more as I lowered my head and suckled each one, trying to go slow with her.

She arched her back and grasped the back of my head to get me even closer. "Yes," she breathed out softly.

Her skin was warm and silky, and I couldn't get enough of touching her. I heard her breathing hitch as I nipped and licked my way down her belly, teasing her as much as possible.

Remember she's a virgin, Blake. Remember!

My cock was pulsating with need as I finally had my head between her thighs, exactly where I wanted to be. Her needy scent intoxicated me as I breathed her in and then slid my tongue between her folds, parting her thighs wider as I found her engorged clit.

"Oh, my God. What are you doing?" Harper squealed.

Her voice was more aroused than upset, so I ignored her question, delving my tongue deeper so I could flick more pressure over the tiny bundle of nerves that I knew would send her over the edge.

I eagerly lapped at her pussy, getting off on her moans of pleasure as I consumed her arousal, getting drunk on the taste, feel, and sound of Harper.

Easing my index finger inside her sheath, I was taken aback by how tight she was, but it didn't stop me from imagining her slick heat wrapped around my cock. She started rocking her hips as I slipped in another finger, trying to stretch her tight little pussy wide enough to eventually take me.

In and out. In and out. My tongue kept teasing her sensitive nub as my fingers fucked her gently.

I felt triumphant as she gripped my hair and pushed my head harder between her thighs, her moans growing louder and louder.

"Please. Let me come," she panted.

I loved hearing her beg, but I also wanted to grant her request more than I wanted to take another breath.

She ground her pussy against my face and I kept diving in harder and harder with my tongue and fingers, giving her the pressure she needed to climax.

"Yesssss!" She screamed as her body came apart, her grip on my hair painful as she came, her channel clamping down hard on my pumping fingers.

I soothed her quivering flesh with my tongue as she spiraled down from her high, sliding up beside her only when I knew the waves of pleasure had stopped.

She wrapped her arms around me and squeezed. "I can't believe you did that. I thought most guys hated it."

I didn't answer. I kissed her, letting her taste herself on my lips before I had to come up for air. "How could any guy hate something that tastes that good?" I teased.

"It was amazing," she said breathlessly. "I've never come like that."

"So some guy has made you come," I growled playfully, although I wasn't all that thrilled about any other male touching her.

"No. But I do masturbate," she said bluntly. "Everybody does."

I smirked, definitely loving the thought of Harper getting herself off.

"Me, too," I answered huskily. "But it's no substitute for this."

"I wouldn't know," she said suggestively.

"You will," I answered hoarsely as I knelt on the bed to unzip my jeans.

"No. Let me," Harper said as she sat up and brushed my hands away. "Let me touch you."

Fuck knew I wanted her to explore all she wanted, but I wasn't going to be able to take much of feeling those soft hands on my rock-hard cock. Reaching my hand into my pocket, I pulled out a condom that I'd been carrying in my wallet for months. Maybe it had been subconscious or just wishful thinking, but I'd taken it out and put it in my front pocket before we'd gone out to eat.

Harper put her hands on my shoulders and smoothed them down over my chest. "You're so gorgeous," she said in an awed voice.

Oh fuck, I was toast. The sound of innocence in her voice was making me come unraveled.

"I love how built you are, but without the bulging, bodybuilder kind of muscles," Harper continued as she finished unzipping my fly.

"Martial arts," I told her, my mind completely focused on what she was doing with her hands. "I've practiced since I was a kid."

She had my jeans down to my thighs without much of a struggle, and my dick was finally liberated and freed.

"Oh, my," she said in that awed voice again. "This is…big."

"I'm big all over," I explained, almost feeling bad because I definitely had an above average-sized dick.

She tried to wrap her fingers around me, but she couldn't quite get there. After that, she stroked the soft skin of my shaft, and then ran her thumb over the sensitive head, swiping a bead of moisture across the tip.

I had to bite my fucking lip to keep from stopping her. "If you keep touching me, I'm not going to survive, baby," I said coarsely.

Starting at the root, Harper ran her fingers all the way up the shaft and back down again. I knew it was deliberate. She was trying to tease me. And by God, it worked.

"No more," I grumbled as I pinned her under me and restrained her wrists over her head. "Prick tease," I accused.

"I've never teased a prick," she answered with curiosity and humor in her tone.

"I can't wait anymore, Harper. Now."

"Yes. Please."

I made short work of rolling on my condom, and then returned to her, savoring the feel of her soft, heated flesh beneath me.

I caressed the skin on the inside of her thighs, making her squirm. "There's no easy way to do this. It's probably going to hurt."

My gut was aching with need, and my cock was pleading with me to bury myself deep inside her, but the last thing I wanted was to hurt her.

"I don't give a damn," she answered firmly. "Fuck me now. Right now."

I grinned at her demand, then bent down to lower my mouth to hers. The embrace became red hot in seconds, her tongue demanding as it dueled with mine. I broke off the kiss and nipped at the sensitive skin of her neck then ran my tongue over the flesh.

I reached down and positioned myself, and then entered her in one hard thrust. Every muscle in my body was tight as I forced myself to stay still while her muscles slowly stretched to accommodate my size. I'd never been with a virgin, but I thought it was better to just get the initial pain over with and done.

I'd felt the resistance, and then the give of her flesh as I'd gone where no guy had ever been.

It was the most fucking amazing thing I'd ever experienced.

Until I'd heard her squeal of pain.

"Harper! Talk to me. Are you okay?" I asked anxiously, nuzzling my face against her neck.

"Your dick is too big," she complained as she panted.

I couldn't help myself. I laughed. "I've never had that complaint before, baby."

"Then I'll be the first one to bitch," she answered haughtily. "It's too big."

Some of Harper's spark was back, and I couldn't say I wasn't happy to see it. I rolled my hips just a little. "You won't be saying that from now on."

"I will," she argued, but the tone of her voice had changed from one of pain to one of uncertainty.

I kept nibbling at her neck as I slowly pulled back and gently buried myself inside her again. "Won't," I said with a deep groan, relishing her tight inner muscles as they clamped down on my cock.

Harper slid her arms around my neck as she replied, "Then show me."

"You okay now?" *Fuck! Please, let her be fine now.*

"I think so."

Her grip tightened around my neck, and I started an easy rhythm, trying like hell to be gentle when all I wanted to do was fuck her until we were both exhausted and sated.

"Nice," she mumbled as she lifted her legs and wrapped them around my waist instinctively.

My goddamn fantasy come to life!

Need ate at my gut as I steadily pumped in and out of her, ignoring the desire to give it to her hard and fast, make sure she knew she was mine. Because after this night, I sure as hell was never going to be able to let her go.

"Harder," she said urgently. "Don't hold back. Please."

"I don't want to hurt you," I grunted, my jaw clenched.

"You'll hurt me if you don't fuck me harder. I need you."

All I had to hear were those three words: *I need you.*

I cupped her ass and gave her exactly what she wanted, exactly what I'd needed since the moment I'd started having fantasies about her.

I pounded into her until my head started to spin, carnal desperation taking over my reason. *Harper Lawson was mine, and nobody was ever going to take her away from me.*

Our bodies moved in sync. She ground up against me as my cock entered her slick, tight sheath. Our sweat-slick bodies slid together erotically as she shuddered beneath me, close to orgasm.

Thrusting an arm between our bodies, I stroked her clit with enough pressure to get her off. "Come for me, Harper. I need you to come."

I could feel the pressure building, my body ready to explode.

Her head thrashed back and forth, and she screamed incoherently. Relief flowed over my body as I felt her climax begin, her nails digging into my back, marking me. And I loved every damn moment of it. Her ferocity and her passion flowed back to me, and I kept thrusting into her over and over, letting her orgasm trigger mine as her already-tight sheath milked my cock.

She clawed at my back as my fiery release rocked my body. Grasping her hair to make her head stop thrashing, I kissed her with a primal intensity that I couldn't control, desperate to somehow mark her as mine.

We laid there in a heap of tangled limbs, both of us trying to catch our breath. I rolled off her, but kept her close to me, my arms tightly around her shaking body as I struggled for air.

Eventually, I had to disentangle myself from her to go to the bathroom and remove my condom, and I frowned as I saw the blood, Harper's blood, on the rubber surface.

I tossed it, feeling both shame and awe that she'd given me something so damn precious.

Me? Blake Colter?

Nobody had ever really given up anything for me, and it made me want to keep Harper close to me just that much more.

Cleaning up quickly, I returned to the bed to find Harper fast asleep, her breathing deep and even. I climbed into the bed carefully, sliding in beside her, trying not to wake her up.

I propped my head up with my elbow on the bed and watched her sleep. Her hair was half covering her face in disarray, but she'd fallen asleep with a sweet smile on her angelic face.

And God, she looked beautiful.

She looked like…she was mine.

I slid under the covers, and Harper instinctively searched me out, sliding a leg across mine and pillowing her head on my chest.

My arms came around her, holding her protectively as she slept. I fell asleep soon after, never moving as my exhausted body gave way to the darkness of sleep.

"You sure you don't want me to go in with you?" I asked Harper anxiously as we pulled up in front of her house.

The storm had passed during the night, and we'd been able to fly back home by helicopter. She lived in the next town over from

Rocky Springs, so we'd driven from the airstrip on Colter property to her house.

She shook her head slowly. "No. This is definitely going to get emotional, and it's something I need to do with my parents."

"Call me then," I said insistently, having already written my number down for her and slipped it into her pocket. I'd entered my own cell into her phone, only half joking when I titled the number "My New Boyfriend."

"I will. Thank you for yesterday and last night." She undid her seat belt and leaned over to kiss me sweetly. "I'll never forget it."

"Not enough," I grumbled, and then pulled her back for a longer, more sensual embrace.

"I'll call you soon," she said breathlessly.

"I hope so," I answered in an intense tone.

I watched as she got out of the car, dressed in another one of my T-shirts under her jacket and a pair of jeans.

"Hey," I called just as she was getting ready to close the passenger door.

"What?" she asked curiously.

"Merry Christmas, Harper."

She gave me a tremulous smile before she replied. "Merry Christmas, Marcus."

It took me a moment to let her comment sink in, and by the time it did, she had already sprinted to the door and was slipping inside.

"Marcus? She thought she was fucking my twin brother?" I mused aloud.

Angry and hurt, I started to go up to her house, and then stopped myself because I knew she'd be having it out with her parents. It was a situation we could easily clear up. But it rankled that the first time she used my first name, she'd used the wrong one. Not that it was her fault. Maybe because I was her first, I was feeling possessive. *Really possessive.*

Granted, my older-brother-by-minutes looked exactly like I did, but I sure as hell didn't want Harper calling me by his name.

Shit! I really should tell her. I don't want her to keep thinking she was with my brother.

I put the car in gear and pulled away from her house, knowing I'd have to resolve the situation quickly, and hoping she'd call me pretty damn soon.

Harper

"I love after-Christmas sales," I told my sister, Danica, as we strolled along Main Street the next day.

I'd already had a very long discussion with my parents, and we'd ended it with a lot of healing tears. They trusted me by returning my car and my credit cards, and I was determined never to take what I had for granted ever again.

I was going to college, and I knew exactly what I wanted to do with my future now.

"You don't seem all that interested in shopping," Dani accused. "Something wrong?"

Before I knew it, I found myself spilling everything that had happened between me and Marcus Colter.

"Call him," Dani urged. "He's probably dying to hear from you."

"I will. I just need to clear my head."

"Harper? Danica?"

My sister and I both turned our heads to see who was calling us. I smiled when I saw that it was Aileen Colter, Marcus's mother. "Hi. It's good to see you again," I answered as we all stood in front of the leather goods store she'd just exited.

After a brief hug, Aileen looked around and then finally sighed. "I wanted you to say hello to my son, Marcus, but it looks like he's… occupied."

My eyes followed her gaze and then landed directly on Marcus Colter. Dressed in a custom suit and tie, he hardly looked like he had yesterday. It took me a moment to realize that he was flirting and kissing a beautiful brunette.

"Obviously," I muttered under my breath. "He looks extremely… busy."

"New girlfriend that he met in college," Aileen explained.

"Great," I replied unenthusiastically.

I felt sick inside, and all I wanted to do was crawl into a hole and stay there.

"He has a girlfriend?" Dani questioned.

"Yes. She's nice. I hope he holds on to this one for a while. Marcus changes girlfriends so often. I don't think he even has time to get to know them."

I couldn't tear my eyes away from the couple, reminded of just how sweet he'd been to me the day before.

"Really, let's not worry about them. I'm sure I'll see him another time." I turned to my sister. "Dani, we need to be going." I knew there was panic in my voice, but I couldn't squelch it.

Dani shot me an understanding look. "I'm ready."

"It was nice seeing you, Aileen."

My sister and I scrambled back to my car and clambered inside. I didn't look back, afraid I'd somehow end up seeing Marcus kissing another woman again, only a night after he'd taken my virginity.

I panted as I grabbed the steering wheel, barely hearing Dani as she told me angrily, "He's an asshole. I can't believe he got all intimate with you when he already had a girlfriend."

"It's fine," I told her stiffly as I started the car. "It's not like he made me any promises."

"It's not fine, and you know it," she answered insistently.

I sat there for a moment, staring straight ahead at the parked car in front of me, my hands still shaking from the shock of seeing Marcus with somebody else. My feelings for him were too new, too fragile, too…important. "You're right," I answered in a tremulous voice. "I'm not fine."

I burst into tears, sobs of betrayal wracking my body as I put my forehead against the steering wheel, my sister trying to comfort me as I let go of all my pain.

Blake

I waited eight fucking days for Harper to call me.

No call.

No visits.

No news at all.

Not a single word came from the female who had rocked my world on Christmas Eve.

I had to head back to campus, but first, I wanted to find out what happened. I needed to know if she was okay.

I'd given her the space she'd asked for. But I was done with keeping my distance.

I knew I was lying to myself about *just* wanting to check on her. Truth was, I needed to see her beautiful face again. I wanted to kiss her good-bye and tell her that I was there to support her if she needed my help.

The primitive male inside me wanted to claim her somehow—before I left Colorado. I wanted to make sure we'd be together, even if there was distance between us for a while.

I rang the doorbell at her house, slightly nervous about how she'd act when she saw me on her doorstep.

Yeah, I'd known she had to have time to work things out with her folks, but I honestly hadn't expected her to take this long to call me. It made me more than a little nervous.

The door swung open, and I looked hopefully at the female who answered. My enthusiasm died out as I recognized her sister, Dani.

I'd always considered Danica to be the "nice" sister. When we'd met as kids, she'd always been nicer and kinder than Harper.

However, the scowl on her face as she looked me up and down with disdain worried me.

"What do *you* want?" she questioned hostilely, like I was her worst enemy.

"I'm on my way back to campus. I wanted to see Harper before I go."

"She's not here. And believe me, the last person she'd want to see is you," she answered angrily.

I frowned. "Why?"

"You broke her heart, asshole," Dani answered, her voice icy with contempt. "You lied to her. You should have told her. We ran into your mother in town. She told us the truth."

Oh. Shit.

My gut turned as I realized that my mother had probably told Harper that it wasn't Marcus who offered to go into Denver to see if he could track her down. It wasn't Marcus who fucked her. It wasn't Marcus who was crazy about her.

"I wanted to tell her—"

"Save it," Dani replied with a protective growl. "She doesn't want to see you again. She'll get over it and find somebody honest. She's changed, and she needs a guy who can appreciate her."

"I care—"

"Bullshit! You don't lie to a woman you care about."

"I didn't really lie. She never asked," I said defensively, wondering how I'd ever considered Dani to be the kinder Lawson sister.

"She shouldn't have *had* to ask," Dani retorted angrily. "She deserves better than you. Go back to campus and fuck every woman there. But leave my sister alone."

I had to step back as Dani slammed the door in my face.

I considered hammering on the wood until she came back and told me where Harper was right now, but then I considered the fact that I really *had* neglected to verify if she knew exactly who was taking her virginity. I knew Marcus and I were identical. It just hadn't occurred to me that she might not know I was…me.

"Fuck!" I cursed aloud as I jogged back to my car, angry at myself for not contacting her sooner. I should have known something was wrong, and every day that passed had me that much more tied up in knots.

I jumped into the car to avoid the bitter-cold winds that were blowing, and started the vehicle.

Hell, she'd been a virgin, and maybe it had been a shock to find out that the guy she'd thought had been her first was really a different guy altogether.

Would she get over it?

Would she eventually call me, understanding that what I did wasn't intentional?

I gunned the engine, sliding a little as I did a U-turn on the icy street.

I'd never been as irrational as I was right now, and I swore to myself right then and there that I'd wait her out. If she didn't call me, I'd try to call her. I could be a stubborn bastard, and I wanted Harper so damn much that I'd wait…even if it took forever until she came around.

I headed back to campus because I had to, never in a million years considering that it would take twelve years until I saw my beautiful Christmas virgin's face again. And that when we finally did meet up, we'd both be very different people and things would never be the same again.

Chapter 1

Harper

Twelve Years Later…

"I don't give a damn if the group is disbanded. Put it back together again. I need you to rescue my sister," I told Marcus Colter irritably.

Honestly, it had taken everything I had to approach Marcus after all these years, but my love for my younger sister was much more important than my pride. So what if we'd had a *thing* over a decade ago? Danica's life was on the line, I desperately wanted her to live, and it made the fact that Marcus had once broken my heart *almost* irrelevant.

"It doesn't work that way," Marcus remarked stoically as he took another sip of whatever amber alcohol was in the tumbler he was drinking from. I rarely drank, so I wasn't exactly a connoisseur of anything alcoholic.

"It *could* work that way. I need you to run one more mission." There was a note of despair in my voice that I hated, but I couldn't back down now.

I'd never begged anyone for anything, and it was especially unpalatable that I had to do it to try to coerce Marcus Colter. I'd worked my butt off to get my education so I'd never have to rely on my deceased parents' money. I didn't ever want to be without a home or the basic necessities in life, and I tried to help the people who didn't have it as good as I did.

So groveling to Marcus Colter after all the years that had passed without seeing him wasn't going over well with me. I'd had to kick myself in the ass to seek him out, and pleading with him went against the grain.

It wasn't that I'd gone back to being the prima donna I'd been before I turned eighteen. In fact, I'd become very independent. My brothers now called me the "quiet sister" and referred to Dani as the "troublemaker." But I was pretty sure that had a lot to do with the professions my sister and I had chosen. Mine was generally something I did pretty much alone. Danica *had* to talk to people about controversial subjects.

Only my family could make me completely let go of my pride, try to forget that Marcus had decimated me twelve years ago, when I was barely an adult.

"Your sister was perfectly aware of the risks," Marcus said unsympathetically.

My youngest sibling, Danica, *had* been aware of the risks when she'd become a foreign correspondent, but she was so damn passionate about her job that she simply didn't care. Now, she'd been captured by terrorists, and after several weeks of begging the government for help, I was running out of options. Apparently, our federal government wasn't even aware she'd been abducted until I approached them and were hesitant to make any hasty moves.

Dammit, the feds were anything *but* fast or foolhardy. I knew damn well my sister could die without some kind of quick intervention, and it didn't seem to be coming soon from Washington.

It wasn't their loved one who might be killed at any moment.

It wasn't their sister, daughter, or friend who could be suffering unspeakable torture right now.

It wasn't one of them who woke up in a cold sweat from dreaming about what might be happening to their sister in hostile territory.

Bastards!

I tried to control my fear and anger as I commented, "Yes. She knew the risks. But that doesn't mean she wants to die or that she deserves to die. All I'm asking you for is one more mission." I was desperate, and Marcus looked completely unmoved, so I decided to mention something I'd sworn I wasn't going to bring up. "Since you took my virginity, then came back to Rocky Springs and your girlfriend like it never happened, I'd think it was the least you could do."

Oh, hell, I was playing my *last* decent card, trying to make Marcus feel guilty enough to put together his disbanded group of guys, PRO—Private Rescue Organization—back together again for one more assignment. It wasn't like I was asking him to regroup forever. I knew that wasn't possible. I just needed him to go out and rescue a captive—my little sister—one more time.

I hadn't wanted to even bring up my past with Marcus. It was the last thing I wanted to discuss. For God's sake, the incident had happened twelve years ago. But I was freaking frantic, and my fear for Dani was likely to make me get down on my knees and beg if necessary.

Thank God I felt absolutely nothing for this man anymore. Before I'd arrived at Marcus's home in Rocky Springs, I'd half feared that I'd still feel that spark of attraction that I'd experienced so many years ago, a flame so hot that I'd had a one-night fling with him, my very first time that I'd never quite forgotten. An occurrence that later had broken my heart.

Now, I felt zilch for the man I was begging to rescue my sister—except impatience. To be quite honest, I found his calm demeanor rather annoying when I was strung so tight I could hardly breathe.

"Could you repeat that?" Marcus asked smoothly.

I glared at him. "No, I won't say it *again*. You know exactly what happened."

If he's trying to get some kind of rise out of me to make me forget my objective, I'm not taking the bait.

"Remind me," he requested.

Like he didn't remember what happened?

If that was true, I'd spend a whole lot of time being hurt when the subject of that pain had thought the incident so insignificant that he couldn't remember the circumstances.

"Just forget it. I shouldn't have even tried to ask you for help," I answered, my tone dripping with disgust.

Bastard! Maybe it *had* happened a long time ago, but I would think indoctrinating me to the pleasures of sex would at least be *somewhat* memorable.

It doesn't matter, Harper.

I had to keep my cool. What had happened between myself and Marcus twelve years ago wasn't important right now. The only reason I'd even mentioned it was to try to make him remember our connection so he'd be motivated enough to save my youngest sibling.

All I wanted was my sister back. I wanted her safely back with me. I worried about Dani every damn time she left the country, and after several years of fretting over her safety, my worst nightmare had become reality.

Dani was taken, kidnapped. Held hostage somewhere in Syria by an unknown rebel group. A rescue in that hostile climate had recently been completed by Special Forces, but Dani wasn't part of the group of hostages recovered.

That made the military all the more certain she wasn't really a prisoner.

My brother, Jett, had gotten some ransom demands, and we were more than willing to pay her captors to get her back. We didn't care if it was another group of rebels in another location, a small group of guerilla fighters the US government wasn't even aware existed. My sister was in danger, and it hadn't mattered what lunatics were holding her. But when it had come time for the meeting to exchange Dani for the money, the rebels hadn't shown up. And no Dani.

Had they already killed her?

Had they not been able to get across the border to meet my brother?

Had they thought it was some kind of trap and decided to ditch the meeting?

Had they misunderstood?

We had never gotten the chance to find out.

Communication had ceased, and I feared my sister might be lost to us forever.

That's when my brother Jett had suggested trying Marcus and PRO. Having once been a member of the private, elite recovery team that Marcus Colter had led, my sibling knew better than anyone just how good they'd been. During their several years of existence, they'd never failed to find a hostage…unless the captive was already dead.

Unfortunately, the group's existence had been exposed, and so had all of the guys on the team. With their identities and private work compromised, they disbanded, and my brother had been one of the injured on their last and only failed mission that had brought them to the attention of the world.

"I didn't exactly say I *wouldn't* help," Marcus finally answered.

"Don't play games with me, Marcus. You'll either rescue Dani or you won't," I told him angrily. This man had toyed with my emotions in the past, and I wasn't about to let it happen again.

I was older, and a hell of a lot wiser.

"Like I said, it's not that simple. Your brother can't go into a rescue situation, and neither can one other guy, our pilot, who used to be a pretty damn important member of our team. Both of them were critical specialists of the group. But I may be able to replace them to attempt this rescue."

I watched him, holding my breath as I saw the contemplative look on his face.

Damn! He was still gorgeous, even if he *was* an asshole. Not that I felt any of the chemistry that we'd had years ago, but in a custom suit and tie, his cropped hair perfectly in place, and a five-o'clock shadow forming on his strong jawline, Marcus Colter *was* aesthetically handsome.

Too bad his gray Colter eyes looked deadly cold.

"Please," I finally begged. "I have to get Dani back alive."

"If I do retrieve her, she needs to keep her ass in the United States," he grumbled. "I see her in just about every damn hot spot I'm in myself. She's a pain in my ass."

"You two have met up?" I asked, interested in how they'd interacted.

Marcus had a pained look on his face as he answered, "Way too many times. If it's an area of the world where there are problems, your little sister is always there."

I knew that Marcus was an international traveler, but I didn't realize he'd ever run into Dani. "That's her job. She's a fantastic reporter," I defended.

Marcus let out a masculine sigh. "She has a goddamn death wish."

I smiled because he sounded so much like my older brothers. They all hated Danica's chosen profession, but nobody had ever been able to hold her back. I didn't like it, either, but I understood that I couldn't stop her from pursuing her passion. It would suck the life right out of her.

"So you'll go?" I asked anxiously.

"As soon as I can get a team together," he agreed, stroking his jaw like he was already thinking about how to organize the group.

"Thank you," I said breathlessly. "I'll owe you for this."

"I think giving me your virginity was quite enough," he answered stiffly.

"I thought you didn't remember," I accused, meeting his steely-eyed gaze as he leaned against the desk in his home office.

"It might be coming back to me," he said absently.

"I'm sorry it wasn't important enough for you to recall immediately," I replied sarcastically. In reality, it hurt that he didn't remember something that had been so significant to me. But he obviously hadn't cared enough to even recall the encounter.

He looked me up and down with a slightly mischievous grin. "Oh, I'm pretty sure it was memorable."

I wasn't quite certain what he meant, but as I continued to lock eyes with him, I was relieved that I still felt absolutely nothing.

My memories were all that was left of what happened between us. *This* Marcus was not the same young man I'd met up with years ago.

Oh, he was still handsome, but he had a rough, brutal edge to him that made me slightly uncomfortable. I couldn't imagine him as the same guy who'd grinned at me like a mischievous boy, and made me smile at a time when I'd been so unhappy.

For a brief moment, I grieved for the young man he used to be. But then, I realized I'd changed over the years myself.

He was a product of the adult life he'd led, and so was I. Obviously, we were much different people now. In many ways, the disconnection from him made me feel…free.

"How did you ever end up forming a rescue group, anyway?" I asked curiously.

Before my parents had died in an auto accident seven years ago, my mother had kept me up on all that was happening with the Colters.

Not that I'd really cared. I wasn't close to any of them.

Okay…maybe I *did* listen, but she spoke very little about Marcus because he was usually gone. I'd heard more about Tate, Chloe, or Zane. Once in a while she'd mention Blake, but he hadn't become a member of the Senate before my mom and dad had died. He'd served a term in the House, but gave up his seat afterward to run for senator when he hit the minimum age requirement.

Blake Colter was probably one of the most politically ambitious men I'd ever seen, and he was a damn good senator, from what I'd heard. I hadn't seen him since we were kids, but I still felt bad about how terrible I'd treated him when I was a child. I hadn't been kind, but then, I'd been a bitch to almost everyone.

Marcus finally answered, "Are you asking why a bunch of billionaires actually got together to do something decent?" he asked drily.

"No. I'm not surprised at all. After all, Jett was involved. I'm just curious how it even happened. I mean, you travel for your business because you have so many interests internationally. But what prompted you to actually think about doing dangerous things in foreign countries?"

"What caused you to become an architect and give out your services for free to build homeless shelters?" he countered. "It's not exactly something a rich woman would do."

Nice! He'd actually turned my question into a question. It was an excellent evasion tactic, but I wasn't about to tell him so.

"I do other jobs," I answered defensively. "And I think you know why I do it."

Marcus lifted an eyebrow, but he didn't ask anything more about my occupation. "I did it because I understand a lot of the politics and cultures in other countries. Believe it or not, I do have a heart."

Judging by his edgy tone, I wasn't quite sure if there actually was an organ beating in this guy's chest, but I replied, "But it's covert operations. And you were actually the organizer. How does that happen when you're just a businessman checking on his foreign operations?"

Marcus shrugged. "I had all the help I needed from my team. It wasn't that difficult."

His deliberately vague answer irritated me, but if he didn't want to talk about his private life, I wasn't going to push it. I needed him for one thing: to rescue my sister.

It had been twelve years since he'd taken my virginity, and we didn't exactly need to get to know each other again. We just needed to get along.

I fidgeted in my spot several feet away from him, shifting my weight from one leg to another. "So do you have an idea when you can leave?"

"We need some intel first," he explained. "I'll talk to Jett and see what his instincts are about where she might be and who is holding her while I get things together. It won't be long. A day or two at most."

Right now, even twenty-four hours seemed like a lifetime, but I nodded my agreement. *Really, what choice did I have?* Besides, his answer made sense. There was no way a small team could go bursting into a dangerous country without gathering knowledge and making a plan. The last thing they'd probably want was to draw attention to themselves.

"Please bring her back alive," I pleaded, tears starting to form in my eyes.

He nodded sharply. "I'll do my best."

I turned to walk out of his office, and I'd reached the door when he called, "Harper?"

I turned for a moment to look at him. "Yes?"

"I'm sorry about what happened. I mean, I'm not sorry it happened, but I never meant to hurt you."

It was all water under the bridge for me now, so I answered, "It's no big deal. I just wished you would have told me you had a girlfriend. You did hurt me back then, but I've been over it for years."

That wasn't exactly the truth, but I'd definitely mellowed out about it since I'd walked through his door only minutes ago. Surprisingly, I didn't even feel a twinge of the same attraction I'd felt for him back then.

"I'm still apologizing for what happened. I was young and stupid," he said gruffly.

"No need. I really am over it," I answered nonchalantly as I opened the door and sped through it, closing his office door behind me.

I made it outside before I smiled broadly. I'd done it, and I *was* finally over Marcus Colter.

No more wondering.

No more shadows hanging over my head.

No more wondering if I'd hold a torch for him forever.

I was free.

If I wasn't so worried about my little sister, I'd be ecstatic.

I sprinted to my rented BMW SUV, a stupid smile lingering on my lips as I hopped inside and started the engine. Late winter was dragging its feet on moving out of Colorado, and the temperatures were still brisk.

As I rubbed my hands together to warm them, I spoke aloud, "It's over. Marcus is in my past."

Maybe the oldest Colter had been every young woman's dream, but he wasn't *my* dream anymore, and I was happy as hell about that.

How long had I hated myself because I still thought about him, even though he was a complete jerk, a womanizer who had barely remembered a night I had never been able to forget?

Oh yeah, I'd tried to despise him, but occasionally, I couldn't help but remember his irresistible grin, his patience, and his kindness that night. Before I'd learned that everything I'd thought was real as an idealistic teenager had been nothing more than a very good act to get himself laid.

I waited for the vehicle to get warm, shivering just a little until I started feeling the heated seats warm up and the vents pumping warm air.

Seeing Marcus now that we were older, I didn't feel a single bit of that old warmth. Apparently, he'd given up hiding behind false charm.

I'd never again have to wonder if I'd feel the same way I did twelve years ago.

I didn't.

The only thing I'd experienced was impatience to get my sister out of danger.

A day or two.

I could wait that long.

"Please stay alive," I whispered to myself. There was no way I could live through something happening to my best friend and little sister. Dani and I had clung to each other most of our lives, and just gotten even closer since my parents had died. She was only a year younger than me, so there was very little difference in our ages, but I'd never stopped thinking of her as my little sister. I was still protective of her, and she still watched out for me.

For some reason, I felt slightly better knowing Marcus was going to be attempting her rescue. I might not like him, but I knew just how good he and his team were once my brother, Jett, had come clean about his involvement with the operation. I just hoped they could find out Dani's location and bring her back quickly.

I sighed, put the vehicle into gear and headed back to the Colter resort lodge where I had gotten myself a room so I could go have my talk with Marcus Colter.

Strangely, I didn't even hate him anymore.

I felt absolutely nothing except hope that he could help me find Dani.

It was a complete relief that Marcus Colter couldn't move me emotionally anymore.

The guy who had taken my virginity was like a stranger to me now, and I was oddly quite okay with that.

Marcus

It hadn't exactly taken a rocket scientist to figure out the supposed connection between myself and Harper. Or rather...*some other guy* and Harper, because I sure as hell hadn't slept with her. I hadn't wanted to ask too many questions, but I was fairly certain that the taker of Harper's virginity had actually been my twin brother, Blake. Who else could it be?

Perhaps I should have set Harper straight immediately, but I wasn't the type of man to make a hasty decision. Blake had obviously had his reasons for doing what he'd done.

Obviously, years ago, my squeaky clean senator sibling had masqueraded as me. The question was...why?

My brother hated being me. Hell, I couldn't blame him. Sometimes I hated being myself, too. Blake had always been the nice guy, the one who would go out of his way to help anybody. Me? I was a selfish prick, and I knew it. I'd accepted it. But I didn't always like it.

In many ways, traveling the world had hardened me, made me less empathetic. If I let every sad situation I saw get to me personally, I'd never survive. If I was like Blake, I would have died of a bleeding heart years ago. So I stopped caring about the things I couldn't control, and I started working on projects where I could make a difference. If that made me an asshole…so be it. If that made me cold, then I could deal with that. What I *couldn't* do was let the horrific things I'd seen destroy me.

I left my office and jogged up the stairs, more than ready to get out of my work attire. I'd barely just gotten back from business in Tokyo when Harper Lawson had showed up, obviously upset and frantic.

As I changed into a pair of jeans and a heavy sweater, I went over our conversation again. I'd learned to store and file information in my memory, so I remembered every word. Maybe I'd given her the impression that I was hesitant to rescue Dani, but in truth, I would have gone after the crazy female correspondent anyway.

I hadn't been exaggerating when I'd told Harper that I saw her sister in almost every hot spot I visited.

No wonder Danica had always hated me. She thinks I took her sister's virginity and then hopped into bed with another woman.

Not that I was ever all that pleasant with anyone, but I'd never been exceptionally rude to Harper's sister…until she'd gotten in a few unwarranted insults the first few times I saw her. After that, it had been open season on pissing each other off as often as possible. I had to admit that seeing Danica Lawson speechless or furious had become a guilty pleasure for me. Fighting with her was almost as good as getting laid. Well, maybe not *as good,* but it was pretty damn entertaining, and very few things actually amused me anymore.

She called me an uptight asshole—an insult which might actually contain a grain of truth.

I told her she was dangerous and brainless because I knew it got her riled up.

Honestly, she was probably one of the craftiest females I'd ever met, but she irritated the hell out of me by being in every place she should be running away from like her ass was on fire.

I could hardly share with Harper that I was a special operative for the CIA. Nobody knew except my family. I'd never considered myself a spy…not exactly. I preferred to think of myself as an intelligence gatherer who just happened to be in a lot of foreign locations and had a ton of informants and contacts in said destinations.

I was no fucking James Bond. I actually *did* have business almost everywhere I went. But I did what I did for the CIA because I was pretty damn tired of watching my friends overseas die in war-torn countries simply because they lived or had business in those places.

My now disbanded group of rescuers, PRO, had been put together because I'd once had friends in need of rescue, several wealthy businessmen who'd been snagged by a group of rebels. I pulled together a mismatched but perfect group of ex-CIA, SEAL, and FBI agents with every specialty I needed to pull off a mission to get my friends out of captivity. They'd survived, and then we'd been asked to pull out others by several different countries.

We'd operated as long as we could before our covers were blown on a shitty mission that never should have happened.

Harper's brother, Jett, had been badly injured. Another member had nearly lost his life, too. Our only option had been to shut down operations. With our identities known, and PRO no longer covert, it was too dangerous for the guys on the team. Besides, I knew if we couldn't operate quietly, we wouldn't be nearly as affective.

Now, I was going to have to try one more time to go somewhere that few people even wanted to be near.

What the hell had Dani been doing in Syria?

She might be brave and reckless, but she wasn't downright stupid. I knew she reported from Turkey, but I'd never known her to cross that line, or even consider it.

Oh hell, yeah. I *was* going to bring her home. But now more than ever, I really needed Blake's help one more time. Luckily, he was home on a late winter break from DC, and I'd have to call on him to cover for me.

I couldn't let anybody know that I was gone. Being away at an unknown destination would be a big red flag that I was on a rescue. As long as I was here in Rocky Springs, or people thought I was, I couldn't be out of the country.

I shook my head as I put on a pair of shoes and grabbed my wallet out of my suit pants, and then stuffed it into the back pocket of my jeans.

I needed to talk to Blake, and I needed to do it now.

The sooner I could get everything organized, the sooner I could get that lunatic female back stateside.

Wondering briefly if I could somehow manage to get her passport pulled for life, I raked a hand through my hair in frustration, more concerned than I probably should be for a woman who readily risked her life to do her job.

Sure, she had known the risks of her job. I never doubted that. But thinking about her in the hands of rebels who'd have not an ounce of remorse for killing her made me move my ass just a little quicker.

I was in my car and on the way to Blake's ranch within minutes.

"When in the hell did you fuck Harper Lawson?" I asked my brother as I made myself a drink in his living room.

I'd gotten to his place in record time. I loved fast vehicles, and I'd driven one of the quickest I owned.

"What?" Blake looked at me with a frown as he plopped onto a sofa.

I could tell my twin had been out on his breeding ranch. His jeans were old and faded, and he was wearing an old sweatshirt that should have been thrown away after he'd finished college.

What in hell he found fascinating about cows, I really couldn't understand.

"You heard me," I said calmly, taking a seat across from him in a recliner. "She came to me for help today. Her sister Dani has been… detained. For some reason, she had the notion that I'd once stripped her of her virginity, and she hates me. What in the hell did you do?"

Blake wasn't known for being a troublemaker, or a ladies' man. In fact, I couldn't remember the last time he'd even had a girlfriend.

If he wasn't in DC taking care of his responsibilities as a senator, he was here at his ranch trying to create new and improved breeds of cattle through his breeding program.

"Years ago," he grumbled. "She was barely an adult."

I raised an eyebrow at his irritated tone. My brother wasn't the type to screw a virgin and walk away. "What happened?"

"Remember the year she ran away from home?"

I nodded. I *did* remember. I'd had a new girlfriend at the time, and the last thing I'd wanted to do was hightail it to Denver in the middle of a storm and leave the beautiful female behind. The girlfriend hadn't lasted with me for very long. Hell, I couldn't even remember her name. But then, none of them ever hung around for more than a month or two.

Blake shifted uncomfortably. "We had to spend the night together once I found her in Denver because of the storm. We had sex. End of story."

Interesting. He doesn't want to talk about what happened with Harper.

I shook my head. "Not *quite* the end of the story. Why does she think it was me?"

"I didn't pretend to be you. She just *assumed* I was you. When I went to see her before I went back to campus, she was gone. I never had a chance to tell her the truth."

"You never saw her again?"

"No," Blake replied in a bitter tone. "I tried to call her for months, but she never answered. I think she finally changed phones or her phone number because it was eventually disconnected."

"Her sister hates me. Harper hates me. I'm assuming that's all about you screwing around with Harper."

"I wasn't just playing with her. She left. She never said good-bye. She never contacted me. How was I supposed to tell her?"

"Well, you're about to get another chance. I have to go on this assignment, Blake. Nobody can know I'm gone."

"Oh, hell no. After the last mission you did with PRO, I thought you were done."

"So you want me to leave Dani in Syria at the mercy of rebels?" I answered casually, surprised at how much emotion I was seeing from Blake, even if it *was* negative. Talking about women was usually the last thing he cared to discuss. And I'd certainly never seen my twin this rattled over a female.

He shook his head slowly. "If something happens to Dani, it would probably kill Harper. But you don't even have a team anymore."

"I'll find one," I answered confidently. I already had a pretty good idea of who I could use to replace my two missing team members, and I knew the other guys would do another mission, especially considering we were going after Danica Lawson. Most of the guys at least knew *of* her, but I was pretty sure most of them were acquainted with her personally, just like I was. She was known for her reporting in dangerous areas, and there wasn't exactly a ton of female foreign correspondents. She was one of the few.

"How in the hell are you even going to get into the country? Jesus, Marcus…this is going to be dangerous."

I shot my twin a half smile. "I've been in worse situations. First, I have to locate Danica."

"I'll help you all I can," Blake agreed reluctantly. "How was Harper?"

The touch of vulnerability in his voice made me survey my brother carefully, and I noticed just how nervous he looked. "Pissed off. Worried. Just the fact that she brought up the fact that I stole her innocence over a decade ago tells me she's desperate."

"*You* didn't," Blake growled. "I did."

Hmmm…he was more than a little touchy about that *subject.* "I know. I would have remembered that incident if it had really been me. She's a beautiful woman." Yeah, I knew I was poking at him, but his annoyed reaction after all the years that had passed baffled me. Hell, he acted like it had just happened yesterday.

"Did you touch her?" he asked in a graveled voice.

"No. But so what if I did? You two aren't exactly together."

Blake shot me a deadly glare. "Don't. Don't mess with her."

I squelched a desire to smirk at him. "I won't. But I'd appreciate it if you cleared my name."

"I'm sorry," Blake answered huskily. "I didn't think she'd ever come back here because her parents are gone, or that I'd ever have to face her again. I didn't think you'd ever see her, either, for that matter." He paused before he asked, "Why didn't you just tell her the truth? You must have known it was me."

I shrugged. "Not my responsibility. I didn't have all the facts, and I didn't want to make her even more angry. Just FYI…I don't know exactly what happened, but she apparently saw me with my then-girlfriend right after you slept with her. She thinks you just used her for a one-nighter, then went back to your girlfriend."

"Shit," Blake exploded. "No wonder she wouldn't talk to me or answer her phone. I should have just tracked her ass down and told her the truth. But I just assumed she regretted what happened, or just wasn't interested in talking to me. I didn't know she saw you with another woman."

"If it makes you feel any better, she's over you. Plus, I wasn't with *another* woman. I was only fucking my girlfriend at the time."

Blake tipped up the drink he'd been holding and swallowed the entire tumbler of fine Scotch. "Doesn't matter. I was over her a long time ago. It was just one night."

I was thinking it must have been one hell of a night for my brother to still react to the incident like it had happened recently. Blake was my identical twin, and we sensed each other's emotions sometimes. For a long time, we'd almost lost that link. But my gut twisted as I saw his tormented expression, connecting with him on a level I hadn't experienced for a long time. "You never got over her."

He shrugged. "There wasn't much I could do but forget about her."

Blake had never forgotten Harper. I was convinced of that. "She's done well for herself, and she does some outstanding work."

I didn't know much about Harper Lawson, but it was no secret that she had dedicated her life to designing her unique buildings, and she was even better known for her contributions to fight homelessness.

"I know. I've seen some stuff about her through the years," Blake said nonchalantly.

More like he'd followed her career. I didn't care what my brother said…he was still raw about his brief affair with Harper, no matter how long ago it may have occurred.

I rose, antsy because I had so much to do. "Be ready to do the switch tomorrow."

Blake stood, and his voice was rough as he called out, "Marcus?"

"Yeah?"

"Be careful. This isn't going to be easy."

I grinned. "I've attempted worse."

"That doesn't make me feel any better," he grumbled.

I just laughed, secretly glad that my twin worried about me. He was the only one who knew about PRO, and only because I'd asked him to be my stand-in a couple of times during our last missions. But I could take care of myself.

I hadn't shared much with my family about my CIA involvement. They only knew the basics, and when they covered for me when Blake and I switched identities, they thought it was because of something I was doing for the CIA. I wasn't about to tell my mother about PRO. She worried quite enough about my safety while I was traveling, especially after she'd found out that I gathered information for the government while I was gone.

I told Blake, "I'll tell everybody about the switch at Mom's family dinner tonight. I'll have to call Zane. He isn't in town."

"I know," Blake confirmed. "I'll call Zane, but you get to break it to Mom that we're switching again."

"I'll tell her tonight," I grumbled, not happy that my mother would worry. Hell, she should be retired, kicking back on her porch and just enjoying life. Instead, she still worked harder than most of us at running the main resort.

"Tomorrow...you're me. I'll be out of here early," I reminded him gruffly, and then exited the room.

I knew I'd told Harper it would take me a day or two to get everything arranged, but I needed to leave late tonight or early morning. I could start arranging a rendezvous with the team now. If I was going to pull Danica Lawson's ass out of the fire, I needed to do it before she got more than a little singed.

Chapter 3

Harper

I took a sip of the wine that Aileen Colter had given me when I'd entered her home, feeling awkward that I'd intruded on a family dinner.

I wasn't family.

I didn't belong here.

I wasn't even a close friend of the Colters, if I wanted to be truthful. Even though my mother and Aileen had been the best of friends for most of their married lives, I didn't really know any of this family well. And I hadn't seen a single one of them since my parents' funeral. Aileen had attended, but her children had either still been in college or out of the area.

I remembered seeing her, talking to her at my mom and dad's service, but now I couldn't remember a single thing she'd said. I'd been too caught up in grief, too shocked that both my mother and father were suddenly gone. One drunk driver seven years ago had successfully wiped out the existence of two people I'd loved with all my heart. I had moments even now when I still couldn't believe they were gone.

I'd run into Aileen earlier at the resort, and she'd invited me to dinner. At the time, I'd thought it would be preferable to stressing out all by myself in my room, but now that Aileen's only daughter, Chloe, had arrived with her husband, Gabe, I felt…uncomfortable.

It wasn't that I didn't *like* Chloe. I just didn't *know* her or her husband. I'd assumed Aileen would be alone. When she'd invited me, I also hadn't known that Marcus was expected to show up.

It doesn't matter. Any feelings I may have feared would resurface when I saw him are gone.

I relaxed a little as I remembered my earlier confrontation with the eldest Colter.

Aileen spoke in a genuinely happy voice. "It's so good to see you again, Harper. I'm just sorry so many of the kids aren't around. Zane and Ellie are away. Tate has to go pick up Lara because she has classes tonight, so they can't make it, either." Aileen sighed. "It's pretty rare that all of my children can be in one place at one time."

I smiled at her, angling my body toward her chair as we both sat at the kitchen table with a glass of wine. "It's fine. I feel kind of like I'm intruding," I admitted. "I didn't know it was your family dinner."

From what Aileen had said when I'd first arrived, she did a meal on a weekly basis, and any of her children who could come came over for the event.

"You are not intruding," Aileen said adamantly. "Your mom was my best friend. She'd want me to consider you family. I just wish I'd gotten to know you all better. You look so much like her when she was young."

I swallowed hard, trying not to be touched by the reminder that I had my mother's eyes and some of her features.

"We were all grown by the time they passed," I reminded her.

"I know. And you kids attended different schools than my children. But it was a shame your mom and I couldn't get all of you together more often."

I didn't think it was a tragedy at all that I didn't spend much time with the Colter children. They'd all hate me. I wasn't a very pleasant kid—or teenager for that matter. I'd been spoiled, entitled, and so sheltered by my parents that none of the Colters would have liked me. When I was really young, I vaguely recalled that I used to like having Blake around, but I'd also tormented him. Maybe it was the fact that he tolerated so much of my shit as a child that I'd wanted him to be at any of our family parties.

Then one day, he'd just stopped attending. Not that I could blame him, but I remembered feeling sad that I stopped seeing him.

I took a deep breath before I answered, "It's probably better that you didn't. I was a bit—"

I quickly cut off my curse word and continued, "I was a brat."

Aileen chuckled. "I know. You were a handful as a child. But it's still a shame that my best friend's kids and mine never got to know each other well. You all lived within ten miles of us, but you were assigned to different schools."

"Good thing," I mumbled.

Chloe was pulling something out of the oven as she added, "You couldn't have been that bad."

Gabe was silent as he sat at the other end of the table with a bottle of beer in his hand. I could tell he was listening, but knew nothing about my family.

"Believe me...I was really bad," I confessed loud enough so both Aileen and Chloe could hear me. "I think my parents wanted to protect me, but that concern ended up cutting me off completely from anybody who wasn't as blessed in life as we were. I went to a private school where everyone else was just as privileged as me. I had to grow up to realize that I was actually extremely lucky."

Chloe came and took a seat next to Gabe as she asked, "What changed?"

"When I was eighteen, I decided to run away from home. I got stuck in a blizzard and spent a few days in a homeless shelter. I learned very quickly how badly I *could* have it, and how much I had that I'd run away from because of something stupid."

Aileen opened her mouth to speak, but was halted by the booming sound of a man entering the house.

"Mom?" the husky male voice bellowed.

"In here," Aileen directed.

I was facing the entrance to the kitchen, and I startled as another set of Colter gray eyes settled on my face from the doorway to the room almost immediately. "Marcus?" I asked Aileen.

She shook her head. "Blake." She waved her son over to take a seat next to me. "Blake, come and say hello to our guest. You two know each other."

It was an odd thing for Aileen to say since I hadn't seen Blake since he was a child, but I guess she considered the two of us acquainted.

My eyes locked with his, and I squirmed just a little at the intense gaze he had trained on me as he walked around the table, kissed his mother, and then seated himself next to me. I wondered if he was angry because I had intruded on a family night. Since he was probably in DC a lot because he was a senator, maybe he didn't get to spend much time with his mother and siblings.

"Hello, Harper," he said in a deep, masculine tone that skittered down my spine.

I shifted my body toward him. "Senator," I acknowledged with a nod.

"Blake," he corrected. "We don't exactly stand on formalities in this family."

Gabe snorted at the other end of the table. "We respect Aileen, but otherwise we all give each other hell," he said with laughter in his eyes as Chloe swatted his arm.

Blake was still staring as he held out his hand. "Nice to see you again, Harper."

I put my hand in his with a smile. "Liar," I accused. "I made your life miserable as a kid, and you know it. I very much doubt you're pleased to see me. But don't worry. I did grow up."

Since Blake had only known me as a bratty child, I doubted he'd believe me. My distant memories of him were cringe worthy, even though I'd only been a young child.

His steely gaze swept over me, finally releasing my hand as he said, "So I see. You're definitely…all grown up."

"We all here?" Marcus's booming voice queried from the entrance to the kitchen.

Aileen beamed. "We were just waiting for you," she told her oldest son. "Chloe and I can serve up supper now."

Chloe got up from her seat. "But the men get to do the dishes," she said adamantly, shooting a mischievous look at Gabe.

Chloe's husband shrugged. "Not a problem for me."

"Me, either," Blake seconded, never taking his intense gaze from my face.

"I don't think any of us will argue since we can't cook worth a damn," Marcus added as he bussed his mother's cheek when she stood to get dinner on the table.

"I'll help," I told Aileen hastily, confused by the way my heart was racing under Blake's scrutiny.

I glanced at Marcus and he shot me a warning glance. I wasn't certain what he meant by it, but I certainly wasn't about to share with his family why I was here. I'd told Aileen I just needed a break, and I thought Rocky Springs would be perfect. She hadn't really questioned me about staying at her resort. Aileen knew we had sold my parents' place after they'd died, not a single one of us wanting to keep the home where our parents had been so happy.

It was too painful to be there without them.

I hopped up, grateful to be able to turn my back on Marcus and Blake as I helped Aileen set up dinner. It was more than a little disconcerting seeing the two twins together.

There was no doubt that Blake and Marcus were identical. They'd even dressed in similar clothing: heavy sweaters and a pair of jeans. The only difference was that Marcus had selected a sedate, gray sweater, while Blake was wearing navy blue. At first, I wasn't sure I could tell them apart if I didn't have the identifying sweater colors. But as the meal continued, I realized that the two men were different, even though they physically looked exactly alike.

Blake traded insults with Gabe, making it obvious the two of them were close. Marcus was quiet, observant, his responses to his mother and Chloe straight and to the point.

I spent the majority of time catching up with Aileen over dinner, but I could feel Blake's frequent gaze.

Maybe he still can't stand me because I was so hateful as a kid.

By the time we finished dessert, Blake still hadn't spoken much to me. He'd blatantly ignored me, focusing most of his attention on Gabe.

I wasn't sure exactly why that bothered me, but it rankled that he didn't even attempt to strike up a conversation to be polite. Of course, neither did I because I was too busy wondering why his masculine scent was practically making me salivate. He smelled so damn good, and the heat radiating from his body made me want to move even closer than the cozy table forced us to be.

I wondered if he was feeling as tense as I was, but I discounted the idea. He didn't know me, and I really didn't know him. Sure, I'd slept with his identical twin over a decade ago, but it had never been Marcus's looks that had attracted me. He'd been handsome, but it had been so much more than his attractive face back then that had made me want to be closer to him.

The pull had been almost inexplicable, but that attraction was long gone.

I let out a relieved breath as we all got up to take care of the dishes, despite Chloe's claim that the guys would do the task, and I avoided both Marcus and Blake as I quickly helped load the plates and clear the table.

After that, I made my excuses to Aileen and slipped out the door, doubtful that anybody would even notice that I'd gone.

Blake

Everybody in my family already knew that I was impersonating Marcus, so I had no problem venturing out of his home and heading to the lodge.

I hadn't been happy when I'd returned from a private conversation with Gabe and Chloe to find that Harper had escaped the family dinner early.

Holy hell! Seeing her again had rendered me mute, and I could barely speak to her without blurting out the truth of what had really occurred twelve years ago. I'd ended up focusing my attention on Gabe to keep my mouth shut, but sitting next to Harper after so many years apart hadn't been easy. Especially since I knew she'd been so misinformed.

Maybe she hadn't disliked me.

Maybe she'd just been angry.

Those were questions I'd been dying to ask her, but it wasn't happening in the middle of a family gathering.

I wandered into the lodge of my mom's resort and hot springs, ready to grab some breakfast. Like most of my other brothers, I was a lousy cook and ate out as often as possible.

It was something Marcus would do because he couldn't even boil water as far as I knew, and he took advantage of the breakfast buffet almost every day when he was home.

Good thing…because I'd taken over impersonating my twin several days ago, and I hated it. This wasn't the first time I'd done this for him, but I was determined it would be the last. None of my family knew the truth about the Private Rescue Organization except me. My family, of course, knew exactly who I was, whether I was acting like Marcus or not. Not that I could be as big of a prick as he could, but family just…knew who was who, even though we were identical. Especially my mom. Not once had she failed to recognize which twin she was talking to. However, my family *did* know about Marcus's involvement with the CIA, and we attributed my impersonations to his duties to the government.

I hated being someone I wasn't, and I'd prefer to be at my own home. Since I had to be in DC a large portion of the time, I really appreciated my time in Rocky Springs. Warmer weather would be coming soon, and my heifers would be having their offspring. I was eager to be with my general manager and chief researcher on the ranch right now, preparing for deliveries.

Rescuing Danica is a hell of a lot more important than my cattle right now.

Harper had looked like she was holding it together, but she had to be frantic about her sister's kidnapping. I'd been relieved that she hadn't mentioned the situation to my mother, and my family apparently hadn't said anything to give away the fact that it had been me and not Marcus who had gone to find her in Denver twelve years ago.

I thought back to my conversation with Dani all those years ago. I just wished Danica had mentioned *why* Harper wouldn't want to talk to me.

It was evident that I'd hurt Harper Lawson without even knowing it.

Sitting through a dinner with her next to me had been torture, especially since I hadn't been able to talk about what had happened.

I started serving myself from the long line of breakfast items in the dining room of the lodge, trying not to be incredibly friendly like I normally would. Hell, unlike Marcus, I actually liked people. And I loved Colorado. As a senator, it was natural for me to strike up a conversation nearly everywhere I went.

But Marcus wasn't one to speak unless he felt it was necessary.

My brother avoided close relationships and was about as secretive as a man could get.

So, even though it pained me, I ignored the older woman who smiled at me as I piled eggs on my plate, and didn't say a word to the elderly gentleman spearing some sausage.

Because it was exactly what Marcus would do.

I wasn't positive where my older twin was now, but I was hoping he'd bring Danica back pretty damn soon. Being Marcus was going against my own nature, and I had to be aware of who I was pretending to be every moment that I was masquerading as my twin.

Now that I understood what had happened twelve years ago, I was having a hard time not setting the record straight with Harper. Our family dinner had been awkward enough, and I'd hardly gotten through it without dragging her away so I could explain everything that had happened. Somehow, I needed to close that miserable chapter in my life. But I'd decided I should probably wait until Dani was back home and safe. It would probably be wise to avoid Harper until then.

Since Marcus said Harper was over the whole experience, it probably wasn't important enough to her to justify seeking her out now.

Sitting next to her at Mom's dinner, not saying a word, had been one of the hardest things I'd ever done. But it hadn't been the time or place to explain, and I had no idea how she'd react. The best I'd been able to do was pretend I didn't care.

Unfortunately, Harper still affected me just as much as she had twelve years ago, and it had taken everything I had not to talk to her. Maybe for her, the incident was forgotten and in the past. But

I'd never forgotten her, or gotten over the fact that she'd completely dumped me.

Sure, I got it *now,* but plenty of years had gone by that I'd resented her for just coldly ignoring me after I'd made it clear I wanted to hear from her, and I'd often wondered why she'd refused to speak to me.

Now that I knew I'd unintentionally hurt her, it was killing me. I should have followed my instincts back then and tracked her down, demanded an answer. But her rejection had stung and it had been painful enough to keep me away.

Now that I knew the truth, I had so many things I wanted to say to her. I wanted to know exactly how she'd gotten to where she was in her career right now. I wanted to tell her how sorry I was that she'd lost her parents even before she'd finished college.

I didn't need to ask her why she was involved in helping the homeless. I knew why.

Mostly, I wanted to be able to forget her completely, because I never really had.

I *still* thought about her. But I didn't fantasize about her the way I used to. Well, okay, maybe I *did,* but not quite as often anymore. If I occasionally read stories about her building homeless shelters, and saw her picture, it was just curiosity—at least that's what I told myself.

The first few years had been hell. I'd been telling Marcus the truth when I'd confessed that I'd called her. What I hadn't told him is that I'd been obsessed with talking to her, so I'd phoned several times a day.

Over and over.

Hoping she'd finally answer—even if it was just to get rid of me.

When her phone number had finally been disconnected, I'd nearly lost it. But I eventually withdrew. If there was one thing I'd learned by being in politics, it was to fight the fights I could actually win. Not that I didn't try to change things that I thought were wrong, but I had to prioritize. Harper Lawson had been a "no-win" situation back then. Even if she had answered my calls, what would I have said to her if she wasn't interested? It was something I'd had to just accept.

"Marcus?" I heard the confused female voice from behind me, and my body tensed.

It was a voice I hadn't heard in years except for the few words we'd exchanged at dinner, and I was suddenly tempted to ignore it.

Harper. What in the hell is she doing here? It hadn't really occurred to me that she was probably staying here since she no longer had family or a home in the area. But it was logical. She'd obviously run into my mom, and it made sense that Harper was probably staying here.

In the end, I had to turn and face her, but when I did, it was like getting body-slammed by a linebacker.

Christ! She really hadn't changed much. She was just as beautiful as she'd always been, a fact that had affected me so violently when I'd seen her at my mother's place that I'd had to turn my focus elsewhere unless I wanted to become a babbling idiot.

"Yes?" I lifted an arrogant eyebrow in a Marcus sort of way.

"Why are you still here? I thought you were already gone to get Dani," she said in a breathless voice that had me hard in an instant.

"Not yet," I hedged. "But we'll find her." I turned away and sought out a table.

I couldn't talk to her.

Not here.

Not now.

Unfortunately, she wasn't about to give me a moment of peace.

Harper sat her coffee down and helped herself to a bagel before she came and sat right across from me, totally ruining my appetite.

My gut was tied in knots as I met her questioning gaze straight on.

"What did you find out? Do you know where Dani is? Did you find new team members?"

Her tone was urgent, and I wanted to spill everything I knew, including my identity, almost immediately.

But it still wasn't the time and place for me to blurt out the truth.

"Not much. Not yet. And yes, I did get a team together."

Harper rolled her eyes as she took a bite of her bagel. "Then shouldn't you think about a plan of attack?"

She took a sip of her coffee, which I noticed she still took black.

"We're working as quickly as possible," I answered blandly. "We haven't located her yet. We can't go blazing into an area like that without knowing where we're going."

Honestly, I had no fucking idea if Marcus had located Dani, but I hoped that he had.

Harper blew out a large breath of frustration. "I'm sorry. I just want my sister back."

"I know," I returned stoically. "Are you staying here?"

"Yeah. We sold my parents' home after they died."

I nodded. "I know. I'm sorry about your loss. Your parents were good people. My mom was torn up when they died." I hesitated before asking, "Where are you living now?"

"California," she answered. "But I spend a lot of time traveling for my job."

"Architect, right?" I knew damn well what she did for a living, but I was so damn edgy that I needed to keep making small talk.

Really, all I wanted to do was comfort her, be there because she needed somebody, and underneath her demanding but concerned demeanor, I somehow knew she felt lost and alone. But I didn't want to risk blowing my cover in public.

Not here.

Not now.

She stopped eating to eye me carefully, and I squirmed under her examination. "Yeah. I'm an architect," she answered cautiously. "But you already mentioned it. When I first saw you, remember?"

Hell, no, I didn't remember. She'd been talking to *Marcus,* not me. "Sorry," I muttered awkwardly. For a politician, I certainly wasn't thinking quickly to wiggle out of uncomfortable questions. I usually had quick answers and a charming smile, but my brain seemed to be disconnected when it came to Harper.

I looked directly at her, and she pinned me with her green-eyed gaze. For a moment, time stopped, and I still remembered how she'd looked at me twelve years ago.

Even in her frantic state, she still looked like the same Harper, her emotions showing in her expression and the depth of her eyes. She'd matured well, and she was now definitely a woman instead of a girl, but I could still see remnants of the eighteen-year-old Harper I'd cared about so much.

Her beautiful, blonde hair was clipped to the back of her head, and a few locks had already escaped their confinement and framed her face. The gorgeous emerald eyes I remembered were just as vivid as ever, especially right now with her emotions so close to the surface. I could tell she was scared, but she wasn't hysterical. "You look really good. Are you happy?" I asked huskily, unable to stop staring at her.

I doubted that was a question Marcus would ask, but I didn't give a shit. I had to know.

She blinked hard and then turned her eyes back to her half-eaten bagel. "Yes. For the most part. I miss my family, and I've worried about Dani from the moment she'd decided to fly toward danger instead of away from it. But I love what I do."

"The commissions or the charitable stuff?" I asked curiously.

"Both," she admitted, pulling off small chunks from the bagel and popping them into her mouth. "Are *you* happy? You seem to travel around as much as my sister."

I shrugged. "I guess I could give the same answer you did…most of the time. Traveling gets old."

I was mostly on the move from Colorado to Washington, but not really having a permanent home did get monotonous sometimes.

"I don't mind it so much," Harper said thoughtfully. "I guess I enjoy seeing different places."

I ate while I watched her, mesmerized by how little she'd changed physically. "Why did you never answer my calls?" I blurted out without filtering my words, but my gut was burning to know.

She looked up at me in surprise. "I thought you didn't really remember much that happened back then."

"I lied," I shot back immediately. "I remember every single detail, and there hasn't been a day when I didn't think about you, Harper."

She lifted an angry brow. "Were you thinking about me when you were kissing your girlfriend the day after you fucked me?" she asked bluntly.

"Yes," I answered, knowing it didn't sound good. But I didn't give a damn. I was never going to lie to Harper again or even avoid the truth if she asked me.

The two of us had been through twelve years of lies and misunderstandings. Maybe it should have all been forgotten, but it had eaten at me more than I cared to admit, and it was going to end.

It was fucking killing me not to tell her that I wasn't Marcus, and it made my gut hurt to let her keep thinking I was my brother. But I didn't dare utter a word right now about the fact that it had never been Marcus who had touched her. It had never been my sibling who had the privilege of being her first man.

Just once, I wanted to hear her say my name out loud, acknowledge exactly who had made her come so volatilely that night twelve years ago.

But I couldn't. Not with her sister's life hanging in the balance. Marcus needed to get to Dani without anybody knowing he was even gone. No doubt he was already in the Middle East, and it was probably safe to confess. But I needed to do it in a controlled atmosphere.

I despised the deception, and I couldn't blame Harper for hating me. If I had been in her position twelve years ago, and I'd seen her hanging on another man right after we'd been together, I probably would have wanted to go ape shit crazy all over his ass.

Harper obviously hadn't confronted Marcus back then or said a word. She'd just quietly slipped away, just like she'd done when I'd seen her at Mom's dinner. I *hadn't* seen her leave, but it had taken everything I had not to find out where she was and go after her when she'd silently disappeared after dinner at Mom's house.

"Where is your girlfriend now?" Harper asked haughtily.

"Gone. I don't even remember her name." It was the truth. Marcus had so many girlfriends that I had never gotten to know the large majority of them.

Keeping women was *not* his strong suit. No female had ever taken priority over business for him, and it didn't take his women very long to realize that they took a back seat to Marcus's other interests.

Harper shrugged. "It doesn't matter. It was a long time ago, and there's nothing between us anymore."

"Bullshit," I challenged her hoarsely. There were sparks flying everywhere, and I kept wondering if one of them would light the flame between us that would blow up the whole damn resort. "Are you seeing anybody?"

I watched her fumble with the last of her bagel and then finally set it back down on the plate. "I'm not sure that's any of your business. I came to you to ask for your help in finding my sister."

"Tell me anyway. Humor me."

"Not that it's any of your concern, but no, I'm not seeing anybody at the moment."

My body relaxed. "Thanks. If it means anything, I'm not in a relationship, either."

"It doesn't," she said flatly. "It doesn't matter anymore. I just want to concentrate on finding Danica.

"It matters," I answered flatly.

"Marcus, I don't give a damn about anything you do or have outside of the skills you possess to rescue my sister," Harper said icily.

"You're still attracted to me. It doesn't matter how much time has passed," I told her confidently. Hell, I could cut the tension between us with a knife, and it wasn't all about her hating me.

I watched her swallow hard, trying to hide it. But I knew damn well I wasn't feeling this kind of attraction alone, just like I'd known it twelve years ago.

I just wanted her to admit it. I needed to hear her say it.

"I told you when we talked about Dani that I didn't feel anything for you anymore. Can't we just drop what happened in the past?"

"Nope," I answered stubbornly.

She'd seen *Marcus* that time. She'd spoken to *Marcus*. Now that she was talking to me for the first time in over a decade, I knew she was feeling differently. I could sense it. I hadn't been sure when I'd seen her at dinner a few nights ago because I'd been too busy trying to hide my own emotions, but I could feel the mutual connection now.

I'd learned to read body language well in my political career. She was…nervous. The kind of nervous you get when you're attracted to somebody but don't want to acknowledge it.

"I'm done here." She stood and then turned toward the elevators to the rooms.

I was right behind her when she stepped into the only open lift.

Harper slammed on the button to her floor, glaring at me as I leaned against the wall of the elevator and crossed my arms.

"Get out," she demanded.

I smirked at her as the doors began to close. "Not until you tell me the truth."

"I already did."

Her unique, seductive scent drove me crazy, and I crowded her into a corner as the elevator doors *clanged* closed.

My patience was at an end, and I pinned her in by placing an arm on each side of her body. "Don't tell me you don't want me anymore. I don't fucking believe it." I was breathing hard as I nuzzled the side of her face, inhaling a fragrance I'd never truly forgot. "Say it," I growled, my dick fighting to be released from the confines of the jeans I was wearing.

"No."

I kissed her temple and let my lips wander down the curve of her jaw, practically drowning in her irresistible essence. "Tell me."

"Go away." She pushed against my chest, but I didn't budge.

Her cheeks were flushed, and I was pretty sure the blush was caused by a healthy mix of anger and lust. "I still want you, Harper. Maybe worse than I did years ago."

"I don't want this. I don't want to want you," she cried out, sounding desperate.

I finally touched my lips to hers, but only lightly. "I'm still waiting."

"Goddammit!" She speared her fingers into my hair and yanked my head down. "For some reason, I want you now, but I didn't want you when I first saw you. And I hate myself for that," she said breathlessly.

My heart was hammering against my chest wall from finally hearing her say she wanted me, even if it wasn't exactly in a complimentary way. Hell, I was taking what I could get, and I couldn't wait another moment to swoop down and claim her delectable mouth.

Chapter 5

Harper

He stopped just a fraction of a distance from my quivering lips, refusing my persuasion for just a moment, and I could feel his heavy breath on my anxious mouth as he growled, "I've waited twelve goddamn years for this."

Although I probably didn't realize it, I'd been waiting, too, and I couldn't stand another second of it. Every inch of my skin had erupted in goose bumps as Marcus claimed my mouth, his hard body pressing into mine with his insistent embrace.

He demanded.

He plundered.

No mercy.

Not that I exactly wanted anything except the ravenous kiss he was laying on me at the moment. I opened to him, wrapping my arms around his neck, and clinging to his big body like he was my lifeline—which was actually exactly what he was at the moment. The one big object keeping me afloat.

I couldn't think.

I couldn't even stay upright without him, and my hands fell to his shoulders to steady myself.

A moan escaped my mouth and vibrated against his as his arms wrapped tightly around me, supporting me more securely, and then exploring down my back and finally coming to rest on my ass.

I let my fingers invade his coarse, thick hair again, my reason leaving my brain as the scorching heat between us exploded into a blaze of white-hot fire.

Our tongues dueled for control, and I didn't give a shit who won. I just wanted…him. I couldn't get close enough, so I squirmed against him, not quite believing what was happening was real.

I'd missed feeling this way. I'd missed the flames he stoked in my body, and in my soul.

Only Marcus could make me forget why I hated him and cause me to melt down into a brainless, molten puddle.

I panted for air as he tore his mouth from mine to explore the sensitive skin of my neck. I tilted my head, silently begging for more, like an addict who couldn't get enough of him.

I can't do this! I can't let my body overcome my common sense, dammit!

Both of us startled as the elevator doors slid open and audible gasps filled the air.

I pushed hard against his chest, and he reluctantly stepped back.

Mortified, I saw the older couple on my floor waiting for the elevator, the silver-haired man and woman gaping at us unabashedly.

"Oh, my God. I'm sorry." I lowered my head and skirted around the obviously appalled couple and walked briskly toward my room.

I needed to get away to think. I couldn't be close to Marcus without losing my mind. I didn't understand what was happening, but I needed space to figure it out.

"Harper! Wait," Marcus instructed when he suddenly sprung out of the elevator and followed me, finally catching my arm as I dug in my pocket for the card key to open the door of my assigned room.

"Stop!" I answered, hating the pleading note in my voice.

Despite my elation after our first meeting because I felt nothing, I realized that I *was* still vulnerable to Marcus, and I hated the loss of power I experienced when he got too close.

I was confused, bewildered as to why my attraction came on so suddenly this morning when I hadn't felt a thing when I'd first spoken to him.

What was happening to me?

"I'm not going to apologize," he said, taking the card from my hand and holding it. "I've needed that for years."

"Then don't say you're sorry. Just leave me the hell alone." He had no reason to screw with me now. "Get your amusement elsewhere. I'm sure there are plenty of women who'd fall at your feet."

Like I'd just done! And my self-loathing was at an all-time high.

But now that my reason was back, I swore I wasn't going to be vulnerable to this man again. Maybe it was just old memories that were messing with my head. It couldn't possibly be *him*. There was nothing I hated more than a guy who couldn't keep his dick in his pants. Marcus was the epitome of a player, a sad mistake I'd made when I was barely an adult.

He was everything I disliked in a man: a cold, ruthless cheater who just wanted to get laid.

"You aren't just *any* woman. I think you know that," he said in a guttural tone.

I plucked my key back from him. "I'm nothing to you anymore, Marcus. I never was."

I opened the door, planning to slam it in his face, but he pushed his way in behind me.

"Leave," I demanded, feeling tears of frustration welling up in my eyes.

I hated him, yet I couldn't ignore the attraction that was still there for me.

The last thing I wanted was to want him. When I'd told him I hated myself for it, I'd been totally sincere.

What woman wouldn't loathe herself for falling into the same trap twice?

It had taken me years not to think about him every single day. I wasn't going there again.

"Not yet. Just hear me out. Please," he said soothingly, like he was trying to talk to a child.

"I have nothing to say. And nothing you have to tell me will change the fact that I can't stand you."

"You want me." He crossed his arms over his chest and lifted an eyebrow, as though he was challenging me to deny his claim.

I leaned against the door, forcing it closed as I faced him. "So what? You're an attractive guy. Does that make you happy? It doesn't mean I like you."

"You'd let me fuck you."

I flinched. He was right. I was so affected by the way he got to me that I probably would have crawled up his body and begged him to satisfy me just moments ago. "Is that all you want? Just like last time? A woman to screw just because you can?"

Marcus blew out a frustrated breath and raked his hand through his hair. "Hell, no. That's *not* all I want."

"By now, I'd hoped that you'd be out of the country, rescuing my sister. Please don't expect me to trade my body for your help." *Is that what he thought? That I'd fuck him to save Dani?* If he thought he could get in a quickie before he left to find my sister, he was out of his mind.

With Marcus, it was hard to tell *what* he was thinking. But I couldn't think of any rational reason why he was pushing this attraction we had.

Realistically, there was nothing I wouldn't do to save my sibling. If it meant entangling myself in a world of hurt one more time, I'd probably do it. But there was no way I'd let Marcus know I was willing to do whatever he wanted if he'd just bring my sister back.

"That's not what I'm asking," he grumbled, and then walked over to the bar in the small living room of the suite to pour himself a drink.

I sighed and dropped my key and the cross-body purse I was wearing onto a small table next to the couch. Afraid of the emotions

Marcus seemed to drag out of me every time I got close to him, I sat down in a chair as far away from the bar as I could get.

"Drink?" he asked quietly, turning for a moment to look at me.

I shook my head, not trusting myself to speak.

Unfortunately, the room was much too small, and I watched him closely as he seated himself on the couch across from me with only a small coffee table between us.

I ran my sweaty palms across the denim of my jeans as I asked nervously, "Then what are you doing? What do you want? Where is my sister?"

He shook his head and then took a slug of the whiskey he was holding. "I don't know. I honestly don't."

"I thought you'd be able to locate her. You have the contacts, and the PRO team is already together, right?" I couldn't understand his lack of urgency. Dani could be—and probably was—in serious danger.

He nodded. "The team is already there, Harper. They might be rescuing her right now. I haven't had a progress report."

I shook my head, confused. *How could the rescue possibly be happening when Marcus wasn't there to lead the team?* "I don't understand. You're the team leader. I was under the impression you'd be going with them."

Panic rose into my throat, and it was clawing at me.

"There's no reason for me to be there. In fact, I'd probably screw up the whole mission."

"You *have* to be there," I said, breathless with anxiety. "They need you. My sister needs you."

"They need *Marcus,*" he answered calmly.

I gaped at him, wondering why he was referring to himself in the third person. "Yes…they need *you.*"

I watched his face as it reflected a variety of emotions before he said carefully, "Harper, I need to tell you something, and I need you to know that Dani's safety depends on how you react to the information."

He looked so serious that I nodded slowly. "I'll do whatever I can to help my sister. You should know that. It's why I came to you in the first place."

"You went to see *Marcus*."

Oh, for God's sake. He was beginning to sound just a little crazy. "Okay. What is it? Tell me." If it had to do with my younger sibling, I wanted to know.

He let out a long masculine sigh as his silver eyes met mine, holding me captive for an instant before he grumbled three words that didn't immediately connect for me.

"I'm. Not. Marcus."

"What?"

"I'm Blake Colter. I'm not Marcus."

His words turned my entire world upside down as I finally figured out exactly what he was saying.

Chapter 6

Harper

I*'m not Marcus.*

Obviously Blake's words made sense. I'd known the Colter family since I was a kid, albeit not all that well, but of course I knew Blake and Marcus were identical twins. I'd just seen the two of them together a few days ago at Aileen's house.

I just hadn't expected one to be the other, discombobulating everything in my brain.

He kept speaking as my mind tried to keep up. "You spoke to Marcus first. He's gone. He went after your sister. He put a team together, and he had to tell my brother, Tate, about PRO because he needed a damn good pilot. Tate is filling in, and he's better than good at flying just about anything that can go airborne, but his specialty is helicopters, which Marcus really needs right now. They're already overseas."

I shook my head. "I don't get it. Why didn't you deny you were Marcus?"

He took another slug from his glass. "Because I'm supposed to be a diversion. Marcus's enemies know about PRO, and he's often watched to see if he's brought the group back together again. He needed time to haul his ass overseas. He still does. I've helped him before, and I'm helping him again because I want him to have every advantage he can get to rescue your sister. I didn't want to say anything downstairs. I wasn't sure how you'd react."

My brain finally caught up, and I stared at him in shock. "You and Marcus trade places? So I asked the real Marcus for help?"

"Yes."

"Did I sleep with you?" I had to ask that question, but somehow I already knew what the answer was going to be.

"Yes. You only called me Colter on that night twelve years ago, and I never knew you didn't know I was Blake until you ran away from the car at your parents' house. I thought about following you, but I knew you needed time to patch things up with your mom and dad back then. So I waited for you to call." He paused to drain the rest of his glass. "You never did call."

Oh, God, so that meant...

"I saw the real Marcus with his girlfriend?"

He nodded. "I was probably home, still waiting for you to contact me."

My hands were actually shaking as I twisted them together nervously.

It made sense...now. But I'd reacted so intensely when I'd seen Marcus all those years ago that I hadn't even considered his twin. "You could have called me. You had my number."

"I did call. Many times, as I'm sure you remember. Before I left to go back to college twelve years ago, I came to your house. I don't remember the whole conversation, but Dani basically told me you hated me because I'd lied to you. I thought you knew by then that I was really Marcus's twin, and you were pissed. She slammed the door in my face before I could get the whole story. Your sister said you were gone."

I sighed. "I was. I left to go to California. I'd made up my mind what I wanted to do with my life, and I wanted to check out Berkeley's architecture program. Dani knows what happened, and she was with me when I saw your mom, Marcus, and his girlfriend."

"I figured," he answered stoically, setting his empty glass down on the coffee table in front of him.

Everything I thought was real had suddenly changed, and I was nauseated by the truth. "I thought you had just played me. We were young."

He shot me a disappointed glance that made my stomach roll even more. "I'd never do that, Harper. That night meant a lot to me."

My eyes grew moist with tears as I realized how badly I'd judged him when he wasn't guilty of anything except bad communication. And honestly, not picking up my phone when he'd called so many times was my fault. "I'm sorry," I said, my voice barely more than a whisper.

"Don't be. We were dumb kids. I should have spoken to you myself."

I smiled weakly. "I didn't make myself all that easy to find."

"You didn't answer your phone," he rumbled.

"I couldn't. I was…hurt."

"I thought you didn't want to talk to me."

"I didn't know you weren't doing a gorgeous brunette the moment we separated," I answered weakly.

"I don't know how you couldn't tell that I was crazy about you," he answered, his voice sounding slightly injured.

"I didn't know," I confessed.

Had I known back then what I knew now, I would have sought him out. Lord knew it had taken me forever just to keep myself from reliving that night with him every single day for years.

The truth sunk in. *I'd slept with US Senator Blake Colter, and not his brother Marcus.* There were so many questions I wanted to ask him now that I had no real reason to hate him. He'd tried to contact me, and my feelings had been pretty raw back then. For years, I'd tried not to remember how betrayed I'd felt by the first man to show me sensual pleasure and an intimacy I'd never experienced again.

"Blake," I murmured, just to hear his name on my lips, testing it to see how it felt.

"That's the first time you've said my name since we were kids," he answered with a grin.

"I was mean to you," I admitted reluctantly.

"Yep. I liked Dani better back then. She was nicer."

I smiled back at him. "She always was. Running away was an eye-opening experience for me. I was a spoiled brat."

"Don't expect me to argue," he replied in a teasing voice.

"I don't." I knew exactly what a bitch I'd been before I'd discovered the world didn't revolve around me at the age of eighteen. Everything had been about me. Thinking about how I'd behaved as a child, and then as a teenager, made me shudder in horror. "I did grow up," I assured him.

"Beautifully," he said smoothly.

My face actually flamed with heat as his eyes traveled over me. I hadn't exactly spent a lot of time during the last decade caring about how I looked or trying to catch a guy. My entire focus had been on my career and my cause to help the homeless.

"So what do we do now?" I answered helplessly. "I've spent twelve years hating you. Well, hating Marcus, I suppose. Then suddenly, everything I thought was right is wrong. In fact, Marcus hardly even knows me. And I'm sure you hated me, too, since you never actually did anything wrong."

"I never hated you, Harper."

"Why? In your mind, I was blowing you off."

He shook his head. "I thought you were angry or disappointed that I wasn't Marcus. I guess you had a right to be. I never told you the truth. But it never occurred to me to doubt that you knew who I was until you called me Marcus right before you ran into the house the day we came back from Denver." He paused before adding, "I think I've been…waiting."

"For…?" I was prompting him to answer.

"You. For another chance."

His answer threw me into a tailspin. I didn't know what to say or what to believe. "It's been twelve years, Blake. It was just one night."

"Maybe for me, that was all it took. I told you that night was special for me. I meant it. Maybe I wasn't consciously waiting for you to come back, but I think some part of me has always kept some hope alive that I'd see you again."

A single tear dropped onto my cheek, and I mourned for what might have been had I not been so quick to jump to conclusions, or had I just once answered his call. I knew I couldn't have a serious relationship with him, but maybe we could have been friends. Maybe the bitterness between us would have been resolved years ago. "I don't know what to say."

"Don't say you're sorry again," he requested. "You have nothing to be sorry about. I didn't realize until Marcus told me what you'd said to him that you'd seen him with somebody else. It would have hurt me back then. I'm sure it was painful for you."

I nodded as I swiped the tear from my face. "It did. I guess it was because you were my first."

"You'll never know how much that meant to me, or how much it tore me up that you wouldn't talk to me again," he answered huskily.

"I wanted it to be you," I said in a barely audible voice. "I knew the feelings were right. I never regretted it, Blake."

"Even when you thought I was playing you?" he asked.

"Not so much *what* had happened, but *why,*" I admitted. "I might have been destroyed when I thought you weren't the man I imagined you were, and I thought my judgment had sucked, but I never really regretted what happened. It was all there for me. The pleasure. The emotions and the pure joy of being intimate with you."

"It was there for me, too," Blake said hoarsely. "Deep inside, you had to have known that."

I shrugged. "I don't think I ever wanted to dig that deep after I hurt so badly when I saw you with another female. But I'm glad I know that now. I'll never regret that you were my first. You made it perfect."

We were both silent, and I watched as Blake took a slug from his drink before setting it on the coffee table.

Finally, he asked, "So tell me why you decided to try to save historic buildings and incorporate them in new facility designs—which I think is brilliant, by the way."

Soon after I'd become an architect, my name had gotten out there in my field when I'd done a design that saved the charm of a historic building, yet allowed for building around it to complete a much-needed structure to get the company progressing.

History versus progress.

Because the company was huge internationally, my design had become well-known. I had inadvertently become the go-to architect for large businesses that wanted to keep some of their history while adding the new facilities that were needed.

I explained the beginning of my story to him while he listened intently.

"You know your charity work is well-known, too," Blake pointed out after I'd finished telling him about my architectural career.

"They're just buildings." I built homeless shelters and supported them wherever I could. "It's not like I need the money, and it doesn't take a lot to make me happy anymore. I left that spoiled teenager behind a long time ago."

Honestly, I got more satisfaction from knowing I'd helped some people sleep warm and dry at night than I would having all that money sitting in the bank. My parents had been as wealthy as the Colters, and they'd left everything to me, Danica, and our three brothers.

While our brothers had taken their money and started high-powered careers, Danica and I had chosen jobs that made us happy.

"Don't pretend like it's nothing," Blake insisted. "Most rich people don't give a damn about the homeless."

I knew what he was saying was true. Some did. Some didn't. I just happened to be a rich person who *did* care. "Most rich people don't care about government service unless it benefits them, either," I pointed out. "You do good things, too, Blake."

He grinned at me. "Maybe. When I don't want to knock some heads together. It's frustrating."

Considering the political climate, I was pretty sure the atmosphere in Washington was anything but pleasant. "I would have been happy if you'd beat some sense into the Congress members who wouldn't approve the funds for mental health care for the homeless," I said lightly.

"I tried," he answered irritably. "Most people have other priorities."

Unfortunately, he was one of a minority who hadn't opposed the funding. "We'll keep trying to get it passed," I said in a mock warning voice.

"I'll help you all I can," he vowed.

I was surprised how comfortable our discussion had become, like two friends getting to know each other again.

Problem was, we were never really friends. We were just two people who'd taken pleasure in each other's bodies when we were young and hormonal.

Now, I was all grown up and terrified that my sister was never going to come back home. Unable to avoid the subject any longer, I asked anxiously, "Do you think Marcus and Tate will really be able to help Dani?"

I could hear the fear in my voice, an uncertainty that was not natural for me.

His gray eyes darkened. "They'll try everything they have to get her out if she's still alive."

That was the possible truth I didn't want to utter, the one thing I couldn't accept. "She can't be dead."

I said the words because I desperately wanted them to be true.

Blake rose and came to sit beside me, taking me into his arms like it was perfectly natural for him. "I hope she's not."

The comforting tone of his voice finally made me crumble. I'd worried for weeks, wondering if Danica was still alive. The stress fracture in my heart finally cracked wide open, and I wept.

Chapter 7

Blake

I felt fucking helpless because all I could really do was hold Harper in my arms as she sobbed out every bit of fear she'd held inside her about her sister's safety.

Hell, I couldn't promise her that Danica was still alive. The international correspondent was in a world where nobody would give a damn if she was beheaded and bled out every ounce of blood into the dirt. Harper's sister lived with that kind of brutality and reality every day while she reported from some of the most hostile destinations on Earth.

The only hope I could give the woman in my arms was a small thing. "There's no official news of her death. If rebels had her and killed her, I think it would be public by now. I've called every damn government official I know to get any news. There's nothing, Harper. Not a single damn word about her fate. Right now, that's actually a good thing."

Her heartbreaking sobs ended, and she rested against my chest as she asked tremulously, "You called?"

"Of course," I answered calmly.

"Thank you for helping. You didn't really need to get involved, and neither did your brothers."

"I wish we'd hear from the bastards who took her," I answered irritably.

To my disappointment, she sat up and swiped the tears from her face. "I haven't heard a thing since they stopped communicating. That worries me."

It scared the hell out of me, too, but I wasn't about to tell Harper about those opinions. This kidnapping hadn't really become public, and I was hoping it didn't. I wanted Marcus and Tate to be able to swoop in and out of there quickly. Dani's best hope was a covert mission that didn't draw attention to the incident at all. "I'll hear from Marcus soon," I assured her, keeping an arm around her trembling body.

I hated this shit. I hated seeing Harper hurting and worried.

"What if he can't get in contact? It could be a remote area."

"He has one of the best satphones ever designed."

My brother had a satellite phone that could work nearly anywhere. In addition to being a thrill seeker, Marcus loved his spy toys.

I felt Harper's body relax. "Okay. So we wait."

Honestly, I'd rather be off rescuing than waiting, but I had a part to play in Dani's rescue. "My family all knows what Marcus is doing. They've known every time we've switched. We might be identical, but our mom and siblings can tell us apart. Outside of the immediate family, it would be better if nobody knows I'm not my twin."

"I won't say a thing. I promise," she said in a strong, determined voice. "I'd do anything to save Dani."

"Including selling your body?" I asked with more than a little annoyance that she'd even consider that a possibility. But she obviously had since she'd mentioned it sarcastically.

"Yes. If necessary," she answered firmly. "And in my defense, I did think you were Marcus. I didn't know what you wanted. So I guess you didn't ever find another obnoxious virgin?"

"I haven't had anybody offer me up their virginity since you used me," I joked, trying to get a rise out of her. She was so damn sad that I wanted to distract her.

"I did not use you," she answered indignantly.

I laughed, a loud booming sound that hadn't come out of my mouth in a long time. "Did you think I was actually going to be able to resist when you practically draped yourself over me, half naked? I was twenty-two."

"I was dressed in one of *your* shirts," she answered defensively.

"Yeah. And very little else," I reminded her.

"Okay, maybe I was a little inexperienced," she admitted reluctantly.

"Are you sure you don't regret it?" Damn! I hadn't wanted to ask that question because I wasn't sure I wanted to hear if her answer changed. But for some odd reason, it was important that I hear her say she didn't have any regrets one more time.

"No."

Her voice was certain and sure, and I let out a large breath I hadn't realized I'd been holding.

"Good." I was pretty damn glad she hadn't answered differently.

"Do you?" she ventured hesitantly.

"No, Harper. Back then, I considered myself the luckiest bastard on the planet."

"And now?"

I grinned at her. "I still consider myself the luckiest bastard on the planet to have been your first."

"I'm glad it was you," she said in a solemn tone.

I sure as hell couldn't say that Harper was the only woman I'd ever had. I'd been a horny little shit before I'd met her. But I could say being with her had profoundly changed me. After Harper, and the way I'd felt with her, no woman could ever touch my soul in the same way.

Covetous emotions seized my heart, squeezing it like it was in a vise as I thought about Harper being with any other man. It didn't matter if a dozen years had gone by without me seeing her.

What in the hell was it that made me feel like she belonged to me just because I'd once made her scream and tremble in a violent climax?

Seeing her again was making me lose my fucking mind.

I stood up suddenly, worried that I couldn't control my caveman instincts to drag Harper away as my very belated prize. *Holy shit!* I was a respected public servant, and all I could think about was getting Harper naked again and keeping her all to myself.

"I'd better get back to my place. I've got some things to work on." In truth, I didn't have a damn thing to do right now except act like Marcus. But being close to Harper was dangerous for me.

I felt like a completely different man when I was around her, and I didn't have a possessive side. Well, I hadn't *thought* I had one until I saw her again. Now I was fighting emotions I hadn't ever been aware existed inside me.

It was a pretty fucking scary experience to realize I had personality traits I'd never experienced before.

Harper was emotionally drained and anxious about Danica.

Now was *not* the time to be thinking about making her come until she screamed my name. And damn…did I want to hear that. I craved her like a drug, and everything inside me wanted to hear my own name while I was fucking her hard and fast, until we were both satiated and too exhausted to move.

She jumped up off the sofa. "Blake?"

My chest ached as she said my name aloud. "Yeah?"

"Thank you," she said softly.

I didn't want her to thank me. "You don't have to thank me for doing the right thing."

"I think I do," she murmured, moving closer and planting a light kiss on my cheek.

I clenched my fists, keeping them at my side when all I wanted was to pin her up against the wall and nail her just as hard as I possibly could. Harper made me feel just a little insane, and I wasn't sure I could control my primitive instincts.

"I'll be in touch," I answered as I abruptly stepped out of her reach.

"I'll make sure I don't give your identity away." She hesitated for a moment before she asked, "Are you okay?"

I turned to look at her. "Yeah. Why?"

"You seem…uncomfortable."

Maybe because I want to fuck you more than I want to take another breath!

I certainly wasn't going to blurt out that little fact at the moment. "I'm fine. I guess I just want you to get to know…me."

At least I was telling her the truth. She'd always seen me as Marcus. I loved my brother, but I didn't want to *be* him. Least of all to Harper.

"I always knew *you*," she answered. "I just never knew your name."

Maybe it sounded weird, but I knew exactly what she was saying, and it made me feel just a little bit lighter. "I don't exactly enjoy being Marcus."

"I'm sure you don't. Is keeping your own identity a problem when you have an identical twin?"

"We're different, even though we look alike."

"I know. I could feel the difference."

"Then you're one of the few who can. Everybody else just looks at us superficially and assumes we're just alike."

Not that there was anything wrong with my brother. In fact, he went out of his way to help the government by being a CIA informant because he thought it was the right thing to do. In his own way, Marcus did his own public service.

I just didn't like it when nobody saw us as separate individuals just because we looked exactly alike.

"You *are* different," Harper observed. "But I'm grateful to both of you and Tate for what you're doing."

I didn't want her gratitude. I wanted something completely different.

I opened the door. "Lock the door, and call the number you have for Marcus if you need anything. I have his phone. I'll let you know as soon as I hear anything."

I left in a hurry, closing the door behind me, but hesitated as I waited for the lock to click behind me. It took a moment, but I finally heard the deadbolt fall into place.

Quickly moving to the elevator, I knew I needed to put some distance between myself and Harper before I completely lost my sanity.

Chapter 8

Harper

Still feeling confused and worried, I'd grabbed my jacket and put on a pair of hiking boots not long after Blake left my room, needing to be somewhere that I didn't feel confined with my own thoughts.

Unfortunately, I hadn't been able to escape my brain, and I was just as anxious several hours later, even after I felt like I'd walked for miles.

I was an experienced hiker, but I realized that I'd just thrown every rule of hiking and navigating out the proverbial window as I'd walked in a daze, paying no attention to anything except my internal thoughts.

Dammit!

I finally became aware of where I was, and eyed the snow that was still on the ground. Spring was coming, but it hadn't arrived yet, and I was cold, following a path that seemed like it led nowhere.

Pines lined the concrete road, and I kept moving when I saw smoke in the distance, fairly certain it was somebody's fireplace, so there had to be people ahead. I kept moving.

Even after hours of thought, I wasn't any closer to understanding how I felt about the fact that Marcus was really Blake, and a completely different person than I'd always thought him to be.

For so long, I'd sucked up every bit of news I could get about Marcus, never realizing that it was Blake that I wanted to know about. Somehow, I thought I should have known that the man I'd been with, joked with, a guy who had intimate knowledge of my body wasn't Marcus Colter. The elder twin was known for never having a girlfriend for more than a short amount of time, and Blake had never come across as a ladies' man—even though he was hotter than an out-of-control wildfire. My mother had spoken fondly about him. Unfortunately, she'd never mentioned that Blake had been the one to come after me in that homeless shelter. Maybe she'd assumed I knew. On the few occasions I'd seen him speak on television, he'd caught my attention, and I'd stupidly been stunned by how much he reminded me of Marcus.

Probably because he was the man I'd slept with!

If I would have listened to my instincts, would I have realized the truth? I'd never know, since I'd been thinking with my broken heart.

One thing I *did* know: I'd never confuse the two of them again. After talking to Blake, and being close to him, my heart would always know him now.

I stopped as I looked up, admiring the beauty of the enormous log cabin in front of me. It was a mansion, but still managed to look cozy somehow. I stared for a long time, going over the complex architecture in my mind, wondering who had done the design. I finally decided it was more important to acknowledge it was a very large but single home in the middle of nowhere, and that I still needed to find my way back to the lodge.

I caught a shadow from the corner of my eye before I heard the excited bark of a dog. I tensed as I realized the enormous German Shepherd was headed in my direction fast, certainly at a pace that I couldn't outrun. I loved dogs, but I wasn't quite sure what to expect from a very large German Shepherd running directly toward me.

"Shep! No! Get back here, you monster!" The female voice was calling from a distance, but the canine stopped in his tracks, and then turned with a disappointed whine back toward the house.

Moving forward, I waved at the beautiful blonde who had raced after the dog, wanting her to know I meant her no harm.

She jogged toward me, stopping just a few feet away. "I'm so sorry. He gets overexcited sometimes. You must be a guest from the lodge. You hiked pretty far."

The woman smiled, and I laughed nervously. "I'm sorry. This is obviously private property. I guess I was lost in thought."

The enormous canine sat at the side of the gorgeous woman, and then looked at me suspiciously.

I held out my hand to let the dog smell it, gratified when he licked my fingers, obviously accepting my presence as friendly.

"It's fine," she assured me. "We just don't get people wandering out here often. I'm Lara Colter."

"Tate's wife?"

Lara looked at me sharply. "Yes. How did you know?"

I knew the ex-Special Forces Colter brother had married a former FBI agent. My brother, Jett, kept me up on Colter news since he'd been a teammate of Marcus's for several years. He'd mentioned the unlikely pair of lovers once or twice. "I'm Harper Lawson. My sister is the reason your husband isn't home right now."

Lara nodded toward the cabin. "Come in, please. I'll get you something warm to drink. You look like you're freezing."

She turned and motioned for the dog to go back to the house, and I followed her.

We were settled into the large but cozy cabin before she spoke again while she was making coffee. Not knowing what else to do, I sat at the table in the nook.

"I'm sorry about your sister," Lara said kindly. "It sucks when an innocent person gets caught up in the craziness of the world."

I sighed. "Your brother-in-law, Marcus, said that Dani knew what she was getting into, and she knew the risks. He was right. She did know. But it doesn't make it any less hard to deal with when she disappears."

"I knew the risks when I was an agent, too. I accepted them. But that didn't mean I wanted some loser to kill me. She does an important job. I love her reporting. She does more than just report the worldwide news. Danica somehow manages to include the human element and toll it takes on the people."

I nodded. "That's the stories she cares about the most. She wants people around the world to know the fallout of any bad situation."

"You're close to your sister?" Lara asked sympathetically as she sat a mug in front of me, and then sat down across from me with her own cup in front of her.

I watched as she doctored her coffee, and then passed the cream and sugar across the table in case I wanted some.

"We're really close," I answered honestly, shaking my head at the offer of anything for my coffee. "She's always been my best friend, even when we were kids."

"I'm sorry," Lara repeated. "I hope the guys can bring her home safely. How are you holding up?"

I realized how nice it was to have somebody who asked about me. I was so used to traveling around that I rarely made good friends. Dani had always been the one I called when I was upset. Now she was gone.

"As well as can be expected, I guess. But I want so badly to hear some kind of news."

Lara took a sip of her coffee before she answered. "I haven't heard anything from Tate or I'd tell you. Honestly, I don't think they'll make contact until they hear something just so they don't draw attention to themselves in any way."

I was slightly relieved that she hadn't heard anything bad. "I feel horrible that I've put your family in danger. I was just...scared. I couldn't get the government to act because she was probably guilty of entering the country despite their warnings."

"That's just it. I don't understand why she did it," Lara mused. "She's an experienced journalist, even though she's young."

I shrugged. "I don't understand, either. I wish I did. Dani's always been fearless, but she's not suicidal. She does exercise some caution and common sense."

"Do you think she was snatched out of Turkey? It's kind of unlikely."

I nodded. "I agree. I don't think she was captured there. Nobody else was taken, as far as I know. And there's a humanitarian mission where she was last seen. She was with them right before she came up missing."

Her phone call from that area before she'd been kidnapped had been the last time I had heard my sister's voice.

"If it makes you feel any better, Marcus didn't have to twist Tate's arm to get him to go. In fact, I think my husband was more than a little ticked at Marcus for not telling Tate about what he was doing earlier with PRO and including him," Lara said with a small smile.

"Why didn't he?"

"I'm sure it was because Marcus wouldn't be able to concentrate if he was worried about his little brother," Lara contemplated. "But Tate would have been pretty enthusiastic if he could fly missions again."

"He's that good?" I asked curiously.

"One of the best, and I'm not just saying that because he's my husband."

"I'm sure you weren't happy about him leaving with Marcus."

Lara shrugged. "I'll worry, but I agreed that he should go. They need to get your sister out of there."

"My brother Jett, was Marcus's tech guy on assignments until the last rescue fell apart. He was wounded pretty badly. I didn't even know PRO existed until that happened. They were pretty secretive because it gave them an advantage."

"Yeah. I think that's why Tate's nose was out of joint. He thought Marcus should have told him."

"I think Jett should have told me and our siblings, too. But he didn't want the word to get out, even if it wasn't intentional."

"Is he looking for your sister?"

"Not physically. He can't. He never completely recovered. He limps now from getting his leg shattered, but he's trying to get any intel he can find."

"Does the rest of your family know?" Lara asked curiously.

"My parents died in a car accident years ago, so there's just me, Dani, and my three brothers. They all know. Jett told them. Since he got injured on the last mission, he didn't have much of a choice. I think they're all trying to get information from different sources. I couldn't wait any longer. I came to ask Marcus to help when we kept hitting brick walls from conventional methods. I didn't realize he'd never told anyone but Blake about PRO. Pretty much all of their covers were blown."

"Only to some of the governments," Lara responded. "Pretty much the very people they didn't want to know about them. Our government didn't leak the information to the general public, so Marcus didn't have to tell Aileen or the rest of the family."

I thought about how worried this woman probably was about her husband, and I felt guilty. "I'm sorry. Really, none of the Colters should have had to get involved."

"I don't blame you," Lara replied softly. "If I had a sibling, I would have asked anyone I knew to try to help. If Tate wasn't perfectly capable, I would probably be more terrified. But he flew dangerous missions for Special Forces. He knows what he's doing. He'll come home safe."

"Thanks. But I don't want to see any of them get hurt."

"So you know the deal with Blake, right?"

"That he's pretending to be Marcus as a decoy?" I questioned, pretty sure that's what she was asking.

"Yeah."

"I know. I saw him this morning. He explained."

After he kissed me senseless in an elevator!

"Do you know Blake and Marcus pretty well?" Lara asked innocently.

I could hardly tell her that Blake took my virginity and I couldn't get near him without wanting to tear his clothes off and experience the pleasure that I already knew he could give my body again. I simply said, "I don't know either one of them very well. I was desperate. Blake and I have some history, but I hardly know Marcus at all."

"What kind of history?" Lara pressed.

"We..." I wasn't sure what to say.

"You had sex with him," Lara accused excitedly. "You're actually blushing. Blake is usually a loner. I've never met a woman he's actually interested in."

I cursed my sense of embarrassment as she laughed. "It was a long time ago, Lara."

"How long?"

"Twelve years," I confessed grudgingly.

"I need to hear this story," Lara pleaded.

With a small sigh, I related what had happened all those years ago. There were no sexual details, but I told her how I'd run away from home, what a bitch I'd always been, and how living for a few days homeless had changed me.

"Why didn't you and Blake stay in touch? You obviously connected, and if anybody needs a woman in his life, it's Blake."

My head jerked up to look at her. I quickly explained the part about the mistaken identity, and then asked Lara, "Why do you think he needs a woman?"

She shrugged. "Because he never seems to be emotionally involved with anybody, he never has a woman at the ranch, and he seems... lonely."

"He's a senator. He's a politician. I'd think he gets plenty of company."

"That's not what I mean. He's an amazing politician, and he doesn't wear his emotions on his sleeve. In that way, he's like Marcus. But I can sense that he isn't completely happy."

"You should be a shrink," I told her jokingly, teasing about the way she seemed to analyze people.

Lara winked. "I'm working on it. One more year of college."

We chatted awhile about her schooling to become a counselor, and the work she wanted to do with domestic abuse.

"That's incredible," I said with some awe in my voice.

"No more fantastic than what you're doing with the homeless," she countered.

I talked enthusiastically about my work for charity, and Lara listened intently.

When I stopped to breathe, Lara commented, with a thoughtful look on her face, "You know, our two causes aren't so different. It's all about people who need a hand up. When all this is over and they find your sister, maybe we can talk about working together."

I was relieved that she sounded so confident that Danica would be found. And I loved the thought of working with her charity. Honestly, there were plenty of women and children who found themselves homeless by trying to get away from domestic abuse.

However, there were logistical problems. "I'd like that. But I live in California...well, for at least *part* of the year. The rest of the time, I'm traveling."

"We work all over the US," she argued.

I smiled at her. "Then I'd love to try."

I left a little later, feeling like I had gotten to know a new friend, and feeling guilty that I'd sent her husband into danger because of my own selfish need, the desperation to get my sister back home alive.

As I headed back down her driveway, following the easy directions Lara had given me after I'd refused a ride back to the lodge, I felt slightly encouraged by her trust in her husband's and Marcus's abilities. She seemed to think Marcus and Tate were up to the task of pulling Dani out of hot water, and since Lara was related to them, I was going to take her word on that.

Chapter 9

Harper

It took me until the following afternoon to completely straighten out my thoughts about Marcus and Blake.

Really, I didn't know Marcus. I'd spoken to him once about Dani, and had seen him a handful of times when I was a kid.

Blake…I knew intimately. Quite literally. And I was getting used to the fact that the guy I'd been with twelve years ago was really Blake.

I sighed as I pulled on a pair of hiking boots. I still hadn't heard a word about my sister, and I was ready to lose it.

Even if the news was bad, something would be better than the limbo I was in right now.

I startled as there was a sudden pounding on the door of my lodge room.

"Harper." It was Blake's voice I heard booming through the thick wood.

Quickly tying off my second boot, I had both feet on the floor in seconds, rushing toward the door to see what Blake had discovered.

I opened the door, panting with worry. "What? What happened?"

Blake stormed into my accommodations without explanation, closing the door behind him. "We need to relocate you," he said without prelude.

I grabbed his arm, clenching at the gorgeous, heavy sweater he was wearing with a pair of jeans. "Why? What's happening? Did you find Dani? Is she alive?"

"She's alive. The government got word of what actually happened, and the press will be swarming this place shortly. Get what you need. I'll have my mom send the rest."

His voice was so urgent that I immediately obeyed his command. He didn't seem worried about anything except me, so I was assuming he had good news. However, my heart was slamming against my sternum as I gathered a few things, stuffed them into my suitcase, then forced it closed. I wanted desperately to know what he'd heard.

Without words, Blake took the small suitcase from me, and then took my hand after I'd grabbed my purse.

"Let's go," he muttered urgently.

I followed him without asking any more questions until we were settled into his vehicle, practically running to keep up with him while he'd strode quickly into the parking lot of the lodge to reach his luxury SUV.

He drove like a maniac, but I soon realized that he knew where he was going and he was a skilled driver, so I was safe.

"Tell me," I begged him as he drove away from the lodge. "Please." I couldn't stand another minute of not knowing what had happened to Dani.

"Your sister's kidnappers sent a video as proof of life. They're demanding the release of some of the members of their organization that we've caught and imprisoned to get her back, along with a boatload of cash."

"I have money. Lots of it. I'll give them anything they want," I told him desperately.

"We can't release the prisoners they want, Harper. They're responsible for taking a lot of lives. Nobody has refused their demands yet, but they will."

Blake's voice was bleak, and since he was a US senator, I knew damn well he'd know what could and couldn't be done. Selfishly, I didn't give a damn who was released to get my sister back. But as an American, I couldn't live with myself if that bargain was struck and those prisoners took more innocent lives.

"What was on the video? How was she?" I asked, pleading for any information I could get.

"I have it. You can see it yourself when we get to my place."

"Is that where we're going?"

"Yeah. I'd prefer to take you to Zane's home because he has a damn fortress. He works with sensitive material and has a home lab. But I live a lot farther out because I wanted acreage. I couldn't get in touch with Zane, and he and Ellie are away right now. So we'll have to settle for my place. At least my home is fenced, and it has a gated entrance. Besides, I'm not sure anyone will even think about going out that far."

"So we aren't going to Marcus's place?"

"No. It's the first place the media will look. His work with recovering kidnapped victims just went public. Dani's jailers mentioned his name in a warning not to come for her. The media will want to see if he's involved."

"So your whole family will find out about PRO?"

Blake nodded sharply. "Unfortunately, yes."

"I don't understand why they don't already know. How could they not? They obviously cover for you two when you've had to cover for Marcus in the past."

"We give them another reason," Blake answered, giving no further information.

"Would the media dare to encroach on private property? The lodge has visiting guests, but the residences of the family are obviously private."

"You'd be surprised," Blake drawled. "Your sister is a journalist. You should understand a reporter's drive to get a scoop."

"But they won't sneak into your property."

"I wouldn't bet on that. They know you're here, or at least that you were. The media somehow got some information about your flight and your trip here to Rocky Springs. If they think you're still around, they'll try whatever they can to talk to you about your sister's capture. I'm hoping between my mother and the rest of my family, they can lead them off our trail. I told them all I'd explain later, but to try to keep the media away with a pretty simple explanation."

"How can they do that?"

"By telling them that Marcus left with you on his private aircraft."

"What about you?"

He grinned. "I'm supposed to be on vacation. Hell, I've taken more fictional vacations since I started being Marcus than I've actually had in my entire life."

My lips formed into a weak smile. Somehow, I didn't see Senator Colter taking many breaks.

We drove much farther than I anticipated, not arriving at the gate of Blake's home for at least fifteen or twenty minutes. "You weren't kidding," I observed. "This almost looks like a ranch."

"It is," he answered matter-of-factly. "Mostly cattle. I have a breeding operation."

"You're a rancher?" Okay, I was just a little bit surprised.

He opened his window and punched in a code to open the gate before he replied, "I think most real cattle operations would call me a breeder and this a hobby ranch. I don't have enough acreage to really run cattle, and that's never what I wanted to do. I'm more interested in producing new breeds."

"I take it you didn't major in political science in college," I said.

He laughed and shook his head as he drove through the gate. "Hell, no. Going into politics wasn't in my life plan. It just…happened. I couldn't stand the little weasel who represented our district, so I ran for the House. After that, I was old enough to make a run for a Senate seat."

"Do you like it?" I wondered aloud.

"Most of the time. At least I can be a voice for the people of Colorado."

I could hear the commitment to doing the best he could as a public servant, and since he was a billionaire who could do most any damn thing he wanted, I couldn't help but admire his dedication.

I crossed my arms over my chest as Blake navigated the long, twisting driveway. "What's it like being an Independent with the political climate being so divided?"

"It's hell," he stated simply. "But I have an obligation to fight for the people of Colorado. Unlike many of my colleagues, I don't give a damn about lobbyists. I'm there to do a job for the voters who trusted me enough to elect me."

"That's refreshing." I didn't mean the comment to be sarcastic in the least, and I hoped Blake didn't take it that way. Honestly, very few representatives gave a damn about their constituents. They cared about gaining and retaining power in DC.

He shrugged. "I try to get out there and talk to as many people as possible, and get as many viewpoints as I can. I actually read scientific reports, and I try to think about future generations."

"You really do care," I stated, knowing there was admiration in my voice. Blake was a rare breed himself when it came to government officials.

"I'm not the only one who does," he said modestly. "The problem is that we're in the minority. I'm already wealthy, and I didn't go to Washington for a power trip. I want to make life better for the people in my state, my country, and the world."

"You almost make me wish I still lived here just so I could vote for you. You're very persuasive, Senator," I teased him.

He pulled his luxury SUV into the garage and killed the engine. He turned his head and caught my gaze. "I can think of things I need from you a lot more than your vote, Harper."

The deep, guttural sound of his voice and his hypnotic stare sent a jolt of gut-wrenching desire through my body, making me realize I wanted a whole lot more from Blake than just his protection.

I wanted...

I needed...

"I'd give it to you anyway," I told him, not sure I was talking about my vote anymore as I got lost in his gorgeous gray eyes.

His expression turned grim as he looked away and opened the car door, reaching in the backseat for my suitcase. "Come on. We'll look at Dani's video."

"I want to see it," I told him anxiously.

"I have it. I haven't seen it yet. It was taken down from the Net almost immediately, but I have a private link."

I scrambled out of the vehicle. "That's how the reporters knew," I guessed. "It was public for a time?"

"For a very short time, yes," he confirmed.

Now everything made sense. If the video had gone public, reporters had obviously gone looking for me in California. When I wasn't available there, somebody found out exactly where I'd traveled.

Damn, it was a little scary how easily a person could be tracked down like a prey animal.

I started moving when I realized Blake was waiting at the open door of the garage, anxious to see my sister's face, even if it was only on a video.

Chapter 10

Harper

Sadly, I didn't have the chance to see Dani's recording immediately. My brothers called me, one right after the other, all of them letting me know not to return to my home in California. My youngest brother, Jett, called me first, informing me that his place was surrounded by reporters, and that he was staying at another, lesser known residence he owned. While I was talking to Jett, my middle brother, Carter, beeped in to tell me the same thing.

My eldest sibling, Mason, called the moment I hung up the phone with Carter, relating the exact same scenario at his house.

Every one of us was being pursued by the media in different locations.

We'd traded information. My brothers, for all their wealth and power, hadn't gotten a fix on Dani's location.

My hopes were still pinned squarely on the success of Marcus's team. Since Jett was the only one who knew what I'd done with Marcus, I'd talked to him the longest. I filled him in on the team's progress, but let him know I hadn't heard any news other than the fact that the group was already overseas tracking Dani.

All of my brothers had already seen the video of my sister, and every one of them warned me not to view it. When I asked them why, not a single one of them had given me a straight answer, so there was no way I was going to miss seeing my sister's face and hearing her voice.

Blake had directed me to a lovely bedroom and dropped my bag inside while I was talking to my brothers, but I'd had very little time to admire the residence.

My main objective was to get more information on my sister, and the minute I'd finished all of my calls, I'd wandered around the house to find Blake.

It took me awhile to figure out that the home was a sprawling ranch style, and all of the bedrooms appeared to be in one very large wing. I wandered into a den, a formal living room, and then what appeared to be a large family room, and I still hadn't seen any sign of Blake.

His house was impressive in size and contents, and I was pretty certain I'd want to see all of it if it wasn't for the fact that I really needed to find its owner. After I'd passed through the enormous kitchen, I found an area with a home theater and an entrance to an indoor pool, which I bypassed.

I was getting frustrated when I finally found Blake in what looked like a large home office, the door open and the man I was seeking sitting behind his desk.

He looked at me when I entered, his eyes troubled.

"What's wrong?" I asked in a nervous tone.

"Dani's video. I'm not sure you really want to see it," he replied grimly.

Hurrying to his side, I could see the video box on the computer screen, but the motion had been halted.

"My brothers tried to tell me the same thing. They've already viewed it. I need to see it," I pleaded, resting a hand on his shoulder.

"She looks like she's been beaten up, Harper. You need to be ready to deal with the fact that she isn't being treated well."

"Show me, Blake. I'm not a child. I want to see my sister," I told him sternly.

Maybe it would be a shock, but I wasn't running away from reality.

He clicked the arrow on the video, making it play.

The picture was grainy, and I didn't understand the language that was voiced over the video, but I watched my sister intently, ignoring the foreign language to look at my sister as Blake increased the picture to a full-sized image.

Her face was bruised and swollen, and her long, beautiful hair that she complained about so often had been hacked off so short that the unseen kidnapper could barely get a hand into it to jerk her head toward the camera.

The video was simply foreign chatter, and the image of my sister being held by her short locks of hair to face the camera.

"Oh, Dani," I murmured in shock, putting my hand to my mouth to keep a hopeless sob from exiting my lips.

I could still see a defiant look in her eyes, and I focused on that, trying to read what she was thinking as the kidnappers rattled on about what I assumed were their demands.

At the end, my sister twisted out of the man's grip on her hair and shouted in English, "Don't do it. Don't let them go. They'll kill me anyway."

The brutal video ended when a fist flew and hit Dani forcefully in the face, knocking her out of the picture.

Blake's office was completely silent after the last yell from one of the men holding my sister captive, probably the same guy who had silenced her.

I walked to the small sofa on the other side of the room and sat, my legs unable to hold me up any longer.

Stunned, I stared at the wall, wondering what in the hell my sister was enduring right now. "How did this happen? Who are the men and why are they brutalizing my sister?" I asked in a monotone voice, trying to separate my emotions from reason, knowing if I let myself go, I'd be swamped in a sea of fear and anxiety that I'd never get back under control.

"Guerilla fighters," Blake answered bleakly. "From what they said, all we can gather is they're acting alone in a small group right now to gain money and the return of some of the men they used to fight under. I don't think they're all that smart. We obviously pulled the plug on their group when we took the leaders. They're desperate to get them back. They threatened to kill Dani if the military or Marcus's rescue group tried anything."

I put my hands to my face and rubbed them over my eyes. I was tired, and I hadn't gotten much sleep since my sister had come up missing. I was exhausted, anxious, and so damn scared that I was having a hard time containing it.

"I don't know what else to do," I told Blake, feeling completely helpless to do anything to get my sister out of the hands of terrorists.

He came and sat beside me. "There is nothing more you can do right now, Harper. Believe me when I say we're doing everything short of releasing those men to get your sister out of there."

"I don't even know why she was there."

"I do," Blake confessed as he rubbed my back soothingly. "Do you want to know why Dani is there right now?"

I looked up at him as tears streamed down my face. I nodded. "Tell me."

"Two American missionaries approached the government yesterday, a husband and wife who had just returned from an assignment in Turkey. According to them, their child and two other teenagers decided to take a joy ride across the border. Your sister followed them, apparently trying to stop them. When it came to a choice between herself and them, Dani waved them back across the border and gave those kids time to escape before she was captured herself while she tried to outrun the kidnappers. She created a distraction."

"Oh, God. That sounds like her," I wailed, letting the heartbreaking sobs leave my body, giving me relief from the pain of knowing that my sister had actually sacrificed herself.

Blake took me in his arms and just held me, letting me release the stress that had been welling up inside me for so long. He spoke low and comforting next to my ear. "She had to have known she was going to be caught. The parents were so grateful that they couldn't stay silent once their kid had told them what happened. They headed back stateside and went immediately to the government. Everybody knows your sister is a hero, but there's only so much we can do."

"So we wait," I stated more calmly.

"If anybody can get her out, Marcus can," Blake assured me. "He's pulled off some pretty incredible rescues."

"I know. Jett told me."

"The government is working on the situation, too. They'll do whatever they can."

Somehow that didn't make me feel much better. The government had failed me so far, but maybe now that they knew for sure that Dani had been taken, the results might be different.

"Is there *any* hope there?" I looked at him, my eyes beseeching him to be honest.

"I've called in every favor I'm owed in Washington, and I've asked every friend I have there to help."

More tears leaked from my eyes as I told him in an unsteady voice, "Thank you."

What else could I say to a man who was trying every resource he had to try to get my sister out of a hostile area alive?

"Not a big deal," he discounted. "Your sister rescued three American kids."

"Dani would never consider herself a hero. Didn't you hear her say not to release any of the prisoners we're holding?"

"I heard her. Does she speak any foreign languages? Any chance she understands what they're saying?"

I nodded. "She understands them. There's very few languages she can't speak, and she spends a lot of time in the Middle East."

"Damn," Blake cursed. "Then she has to believe that they aren't going to let her leave there alive."

"That's what I'm afraid of right now," I confessed breathlessly.

I was so nervous I nearly jumped off the couch as Blake's cell phone rang. I sat up and moved away from him so he could dig in his pocket and answer it.

I watched as his expression grew dim and he gave one-word answers on his end of the line.

Finally, he asked, "So you're going in tomorrow?"

My eyes widened, and I was hoping like hell the call was about Dani. I held my breath, waiting until he hung up to release it. "Was it Marcus?"

Blake nodded. "He found the location. He just needs time to set up the plan."

"Thank God," I said, relief soaking into my body now that I knew somebody was on their way toward my sister's prison. "Does the government know what he's doing?"

Blake was silent for a moment before he answered. "Some of it."

It was a cryptic answer, something I wasn't used to with Blake. He'd handled things pretty honestly with me so far. "What does that mean?"

"That means you don't know everything."

"What?"

He let out a loud, masculine sigh of defeat. "I'm going to tell you something, but it's a fact that nobody knows outside my family. Something I'd never tell anyone I didn't trust."

"I won't say a word. I swear." Anything Blake told me that was personal would go to my grave with me. "I'd never betray your confidence."

"Marcus has other ties to the government. He does special operations for the CIA."

"He's a spy?" It was the last thing I expected to hear.

"He got into it years ago. He came across some sensitive information while he was doing business in another country. Marcus was a legitimate businessman, and he was just there checking on foreign interests. But he couldn't ignore the danger to his own country, so he approached the head of the CIA. Eventually, he was recruited to gather information for the US while he was traveling. He's been a special agent ever since."

Okay. That explained Blake's roundabout answers. "So the CIA knew about PRO?"

"Not for a while. PRO was something Marcus ran independent from the government. He knew they wouldn't officially support what he was doing. Hell, he didn't even want to tell me because I was a senator and he didn't like the conflict of interests it might cause."

"And did it?"

He nodded. "A little. But I supported what Marcus was doing. He saved lives, so I didn't give a shit if the government officially supported it or not. As long as they didn't get in his way, I didn't say anything."

"You aided and abetted him," I said in a hushed tone. "You helped him."

"Officially, no. Unofficially, I did." He shot me a shit-eating grin.

His mischievous smile made my heart skip several beats as I looked into his warm, gray eyes, a gaze so different from Marcus's. The twins might support each other, but they were so completely different, and I saw the young man who I'd cared about so much years ago in Blake's long, fixed stare.

He'd always been warm and sweet, but now that package was in the persona of a powerful man, and it made him even more inviting. "I can't believe you never found a nice girl and got married," I blurted out without thinking.

"I found a nice girl a long time ago. She ran away and dumped me," he said in a deep, sincere voice.

I knew he was talking about me, and I could feel my damn face flame red. "Stupid girl."

"Actually, she was brilliant. I heard she turned into a genius architect who designs extraordinary buildings and gives a lot of her time to building and supporting homeless shelters."

"If I was brilliant, I never would have lost you." My whisper was barely audible, but Blake heard it.

"You never lost me, Harper. I never forgot you." He tucked a wayward strand of hair gently behind my ear.

"I never forgot you, either," I answered quietly. "And believe me, I tried."

"Stop trying," he grumbled.

I laughed because I couldn't help myself. "Believe me, I've given up."

He shot me a disbelieving look. "You're not planning on running away again when all this is over?"

I didn't know exactly what I planned, but I knew forgetting Blake was impossible. "No. I stopped running away from everything that scared me a long time ago."

"Jesus, Harper." He leaned toward me, close enough that I could feel his breath against my lips. "Why didn't I just go track you down?"

"Maybe for the same reason I never answered my phone. I was scared back then, Blake. I didn't want to be with a man who couldn't stay with just one woman."

"I'm not that man."

My heart tripped in response to his sincere vow. I believed him, because from the moment I'd been with Blake twelve years ago, I'd probably known deep down inside that I'd never get over him. "I hated myself for giving my virginity to a player."

"You didn't," he reminded me.

God, I still cared so much about Blake that my heart ached to touch him, but I also knew I could never have a serious relationship with him. I could steal every moment I could get while we were together, or I could run away, which wasn't an option. My running days *were* over.

I didn't want the heartbreaking pain of losing him again, yet I knew I wasn't going to resist taking every moment of pleasure that I could in his company.

Unable to stop myself, I threaded my fingers in his hair and pulled his head down to kiss him, my body aching for something it hadn't experienced in a very long time.

Blake instantly took control of the embrace, pressing his powerful body against me until I was under him, his forceful, dominant persuasion taking over as he pinned my body beneath him while he was still kissing me like he couldn't get enough.

I sighed into his mouth, nipping at his lower lip as he came up air, wanting him to feel every bit of the same all-consuming passion he wrung from me.

One moment, all I could feel was Blake, and the next…he was gone.

Chapter 11

Blake

Moving away from a very needy, lusty Harper was probably the hardest thing I'd ever done.

Still, I had forced myself away from the woman I wanted more than I'd ever wanted anything or anyone in my entire life, and moved across the room. I was sitting on the corner of the desk, my fists clenched and my gaze averted from her tempting figure sprawled out on the small sofa of my office.

It can't happen like this. I can't fuck her when she's vulnerable.

And dammit, I *did* want to strip her naked and take her on the desk, on the floor, up against the wall…it didn't fucking matter where or how it happened. As long as it was hot, fast, and hard.

I needed to claim the woman I'd waited the last twelve years to be with again.

Maybe I hadn't admitted it to myself consciously, but something buried deep inside me knew that nobody except Harper would ever be the woman I wanted.

Had I come close to fucking other women? Hell, yeah.

Had I gone through with it? Hell, no.

Using another female wouldn't have been a damn bit different from getting myself off, which I did pretty damn often.

But Harper had ruined me that Christmas Eve so long ago. The way I'd felt when I was with her was different from anything I'd ever experienced, and I'd never felt that way again.

Sure, I'd had mad crushes on girls *before* Harper. She hadn't been my first, but she'd certainly been my last.

I'd never really examined why I had no desire to screw other women. It was just…there. Harper had wedged her way into my soul in a way I couldn't explain. And the thought seemed so laughable that I'd never even shared how I felt with Marcus, my twin.

I explained it away when I rationalized my behavior to myself.

I was too damn busy.

I was too tired.

I traveled too much.

My lifestyle wasn't conducive to having a relationship.

Bullshit—all of it.

The naked truth was…no other woman made me feel like she did. And if I couldn't have *that,* I wasn't willing to settle for anything else.

Yeah, I realized that some guys didn't need to feel anything except horny to screw another woman. I used to think the same thing.

Until I met Harper.

Until I *had* Harper.

She was mine, and I was convinced it was never supposed to be any other way.

"I can't do this, Harper," I explained in a voice that was still hoarse with raw desire.

"Why?"

I watched her sit up on the couch and run nervous hands down the legs of her jeans. I'd seen her do that before. It was some kind of anxious reaction that made me fucking crazy. Maybe because I wanted to be wrapping those long legs around my waist so I could feel what it was like to bury myself in ecstasy again.

"You're worried about Dani. You're emotionally and physically exhausted." I could see the dark circles beneath her eyes, and her fear made me edgy as hell. I couldn't even think about how I'd survive her grief if Danica didn't make it back stateside alive.

"I am all of those things," she admitted quietly. "But I do want you, Blake."

Maybe I was greedy. Maybe I wanted her full attention. Maybe I wanted her completely focused on me and us. For whatever the reason, the time wasn't right.

"Our timing always did suck," I grumbled.

Harper smiled. "Is there ever a right time?"

"There should be," I said grimly. "But right now you're running on emotion and adrenaline. I'm not going to take advantage of that."

"I should have answered my phone years ago," she said thoughtfully.

"I should have tracked your beautiful ass down when you didn't," I answered regretfully.

I'd subconsciously waited for Harper for twelve damn years, and now we were together out of necessity. It wasn't what I wanted, and it sure as hell wasn't what I needed.

Screwing her right now was never going to get her out of my system. Not after she'd quietly haunted me for so many years.

Yeah, my cock might disagree at the moment, but I wasn't a twenty-two-year-old college kid anymore.

"Are you hungry?" she asked in a more composed voice.

The only thing I really wanted was her, but I answered, "Yes. But for God's sake, don't ask me to cook. Nothing I make would be edible. Why do you think I raid Mom's buffet in the mornings?"

"I thought you were Marcus getting breakfast at the buffet."

"I do the same thing. I can't cook, either," I grumbled.

Her delighted laugh flowed over my senses like warm water after a cold outing. It felt pretty damn good.

She stood, and I surveyed her from a distance, noting how little she'd really changed. Harper had matured, but she was still as gut-wrenchingly beautiful as she'd been at the age of eighteen. She didn't have to be perfectly put together or wear designer clothing with lots of makeup.

Her hair was falling out of its clip.

Her eyes were puffy from crying.

And she wasn't dressed to impress in a pair of jeans, a violet sweater, and her hiking boots.

And dammit, she was more attractive to me than any of the women I'd met who *did* take hours to put themselves together perfectly.

Maybe I was just too accustomed to the DC crowd that Harper's total lack of artifice appealed to me so much that I was desperate to keep her close.

There was more to all this than simple desire or lust, but I couldn't and wouldn't think about it now. I was pretty sure my head would explode.

"I'll cook if you have food," she offered.

"I have no idea what's stocked. I have a housekeeper, but I'm supposed to be on vacation. I'm not sure what's in the freezer."

She walked across the room toward me. "And exactly when were you supposed to return from…where was it? Hawaii? The Caribbean? I suppose it would have to be someplace warm."

She was teasing, and it made my mood lighter. "I don't think we made up a place this time, so pick any of them. Marcus and I didn't have time for a complete façade."

"Some five-star Caribbean resort then," she decided.

"There was no return date mentioned," I said with a small grin. Harper's little game was infectious.

"So I guess I'll see what's stocked up for a guy who might be back…whenever."

She turned and started making her way to the kitchen, and I smirked when she made a wrong turn. "This way," I called after her.

"Dammit. Why do you have to have a house this big?" she mumbled as she brushed past me.

I suddenly remembered what she'd said about my dick being too big years ago. "You got a problem with big?"

She shot me a mischievous look over her shoulder. She knew exactly what I was thinking. "Sometimes I do in the beginning. But it eventually works."

I laughed as I followed her, still damn near intoxicated from the light floral scent she left behind as she moved past me.

I followed her because I couldn't help myself. "So you don't have a big house in California?"

She shook her head as she moved across the kitchen and opened the refrigerator. "I have a condo. There was no point in getting a big house. I'm never home."

I knew damn well Harper was wealthy. Her parents had been as rich as mine. "What happened to the rich girl who used to overspend on her parents' credit cards?"

"She got cured of most of her selfishness by spending a little time with the homeless," Harper answered bluntly. "Now I buy for my needs instead of to impress other people."

I knew all of the things she'd learned from her brief period of homelessness had stuck with her. Harper did more good for people who needed help than almost anyone I knew. "What are you working on now?"

I was curious to see what her latest projects were.

"I have a commissioned job near Boston. So I'm working on a shelter there, too."

"How long are you going to build shelters?" I asked curiously.

Harper pulled some items from the refrigerator, and then looked in the freezer. "As long as there's more than a half million people in this country without a roof over their heads," she answered firmly as she perused my food stock. "Your sister-in-law mentioned that a lot of the women in your family support a domestic abuse charity. I'd like to work with them in the future if I can."

"Do you need funding?" Hell, I'd give her my fortune if I thought it would make her happy.

She shook her head. "Not really. My siblings and I have plenty of funds, but I don't suppose we can go it alone forever."

"I'll help you set up a charity, and it can get continually funded."

She shot me a happy smile. "I'd like that. Maybe I can do more."

Jesus! I loved it when she looked at me like I was her personal superhero just for suggesting I help her in some small way. "You already do a lot. You've done two places in California, right?"

Okay. Yeah. Maybe I'd noticed some of the things Harper had done.

"Yes. One up north, and one in Southern California."

"Don't make yourself crazy. You can't solve the problems all by yourself. Believe me, the government has been trying to improve the issue for years."

She came closer as she dropped some beef on the counter between us. "Not hard enough," she said in a disappointed voice. "A lot of those people don't have the mental capacity to take care of themselves. Some are our veterans who deserve better. And I hate that there are kids and mothers on the streets. The *government* needs to work harder."

"You're right. But getting some of the rich farts in Congress to admit we have a very real homeless problem can be challenging."

Her emerald eyes laughed at me as she asked, "Are you one of those rich farts, Senator Colter?"

"Nope. I might be rich, but I'm not oblivious of the problems in our country."

"Good. Keep it that way," she suggested. "Once they lose touch with their humanity, those representatives are useless."

"Tell me about it," I answered drily. "Sometimes my duties as a senator seem fruitless. But then I'm reminded why I'm there, why I ran for office, and I keep on trying."

Harper filled a pot with water and turned it on high. From looking over the ingredients, I assumed she was making some kind of pasta dish.

She paused and then looked at me as she asked sincerely, "Why *did* you run?"

I smirked at her. "Because there was some rich fart who needed to get ejected from his seat."

"I'm serious."

I shrugged. "So am I. He'd been a politician for too long. Nothing was getting done for the problems we were having in this state. He didn't talk to the farmers, the ranchers, or any of the other people who mattered. He was so enmeshed in DC that he forgot who he was working for and who elected him."

She tilted her head as she surveyed me. "Something tells me you'll never forget."

My heart roared as she looked at me like I was somebody special just because I was doing the work I was supposed to be doing. "If I ever do, I'll exit DC so fast I'll leave a trail of smoke behind me," I vowed. I was in Washington for the people. If I ever got as engrossed with the lobbyists as some of the members of Congress were, so far up their ass that they didn't give a damn what was right and what was wrong, I'd quit.

"So what were your plans when we first met? I never asked you."

"I was getting ready to graduate with my bachelor's. I really thought I wanted to be a veterinarian, but I ended up switching to animal genetics. I'd just gotten my doctorate when I decided to run for Congress."

She laughed as she added pasta to the boiling water. "So you're actually Dr. Senator Colter?"

I grimaced. "Technically, I suppose. I'd prefer to just be Blake most of the time."

"So your genetic study is on hold."

"Not really. I'm working on developing healthier breeds of cattle here at the ranch right now. I have people in charge of the research and jobs while I'm gone, but I do what I can. My sister Chloe is a vet, and her husband, Gabe, is one of my best friends. He breeds horses, so we try to help each other out when we can."

Harper paused what she was doing and moved over to the counter. Placing her elbows on the tile, she stared up at me and said, "You've grown into a pretty amazing man, Blake Colter."

My chest ached, and I wanted to reach out and grab her, drag her over the counter, and then nail her right there on the kitchen cupboard.

Truth was, I thought she'd grown into a pretty amazing woman, too.

And the Harper Lawson she was today was all mine, just like she'd been when she was eighteen.

She just didn't realize it yet.

Chapter 12

Marcus

I fucking hated night operations, but very few rescues could be carried out in the light of day. I could do plenty of information gathering for the CIA during the daylight, but rescues were a whole different story.

I'd broken away from the rest of my team, doing a solo job of finding and pulling Danica out of her prison.

Luckily, she hadn't been taken that far over the border, but we were still in very hostile territory, and the fewer people involved, the better.

I moved through the dusty camp, trying my damnedest not to choke on the dust swirling around in the desert climate.

Dressed completely in black, my eyes adjusted to the bulky night vision goggles I was wearing that made me see most everything in shades of green, I looked among the few tents, which I assumed held the sleeping rebels.

Danica would be held in the most solid structure around, and it didn't take me long to notice the stone building in the center of camp, the tents surrounding the structure like it held priceless items that needed guarding.

To be honest, what was inside meant a whole lot of money and potential power for the terrorists, but those fuckers weren't getting what they wanted.

The government was stalling, and if we didn't get Danica out of this whole damn mess, she'd most likely end up dead.

I wasn't surprised to find an ancient but sturdy lock on the wooden door, and I quickly flipped the lock open with the tools on my belt, and then pushed on it slowly to keep from making a lot of noise.

I couldn't see her well, but I immediately recognized the small figure lying on the dirty floor, her arms around her legs as she curled up in a fetal position to sleep.

I dropped to the ground, and then crawled across the floor, quickly slapping a hand over her mouth. As I expected, she initially struggled, and she wasn't exactly weak. Even though she'd probably been deprived of food, water, and most of the necessities, given enough just to keep her alive, she still fought like a wildcat.

I subdued her, pinning her beneath my body as I tried to make her understand I was there to help. "Danica. It's Marcus Colter. I'm getting you out of here. Stay quiet."

My voice was a harsh whisper, but she immediately stopped fighting. "Marcus?" she whispered weakly.

I put a finger to her lips, then crouched and picked her up, startled by what a lightweight she was right now. The Danica Lawson I was accustomed to was petite, but she was built with a set of curves that were hard to ignore.

Fortunately, she seemed to be coherent enough to understand that I was helping her, and she gently wrapped her arms around my neck as I picked my way out of the camp without making another sound.

I had to haul her body away from the camp, but she was so slight that it wasn't exactly taxing. We made it to the Jeep, and the two men assigned to the escape route started moving the minute we hopped in.

Adrenaline was flowing through my body as we made good time getting to the border, Danica trembling in my arms the entire ride.

She didn't speak.

She didn't move.

All she did was cling to me as we sped toward the border.

I wasn't sure if she was too weak or too scared to make a move, but I was grateful for her silence. All I wanted was to get her the hell into a chopper and hightail it out of the area.

After what seemed like an eternity, we passed over the border and into Turkey, and I wasted no time hopping into the helicopter that Tate had standing by.

Our medic hoisted Danica out of my arms, but I didn't feel relieved. I felt annoyed that I had to let go of her, and I crowded in next to him while he examined her.

The rest of the PRO team clambered into the high-tech bird, and Tate lifted off like a bat out of hell the moment the last guy had piled in.

He was headed for the American embassy, but I wasn't sure if Danica needed medical assistance first.

The medic sat her up and gave her water while still assessing how coherent she was.

She answered his questions, but it was obvious she was weak.

And damn…she was thin.

"You okay?" I asked her as I crouched down beside her.

She nodded as she licked her dry, cracked lips. "Yeah. I'll live. I never thought I'd see the day when I had to thank you for getting me out of that nightmare."

"Don't worry. I'll keep reminding you," I answered drily, but I was actually glad to hear her cynicism. Since it was part of her normal personality, I didn't take offense.

Now that I pretty much understood why she'd hated me from the first time we'd run into each other, I couldn't blame her for her caustic remarks whenever we saw each other.

She thought I'd broken her sister's heart. I suppose that was enough cause to dislike a man, even if she was misinformed.

Danica might annoy me, but even I had to admit that she had spunk. I'd already heard the reason why she'd been captured, and it had taken a lot of guts to give up her own life to save some stupid kids.

As I finally got a clearer look at her face, I felt an unusual anger start to rise, and it kept growing in volume as I examined her bloody, bruised face, and her hacked-off hair. From the way she was holding her ribcage, I assumed she probably had some broken ribs.

Her long, blonde hair was gone, and her eyes looked enormous in her thin face.

"I know I look bad, but I'll live, Colter," she told me stoically.

I nodded sharply, and then told myself she'd definitely stay alive. I wasn't rescuing her ass again.

As the medic tended her injuries, my fury reached an all-time high. Every cut, every bruise, for every fucking time they'd touched her or hurt her, I wanted to give that back to the kidnappers twofold.

Maybe it was a damn good thing I hadn't really been able to see her injuries that well before we left the camp.

Had I known how badly they'd brutalized her, I would have shot every one of the son of a bitches dead without a single ounce of remorse.

Chapter 13

Harper

I woke up screaming, and as I finally became aware of what I was doing, I choked back a sob of fear.

I'd been dreaming about Dani.

I'd seen her beheaded and helpless in my nightmare.

I wrapped my arms around my body to comfort myself, refusing to believe it was a premonition of some kind. I wasn't psychic, and it was just a dream.

"She's okay. She's okay. She's okay." I rocked my body as I chanted the mantra, hoping I'd start to believe it soon.

But it had seemed so real that I felt a sinking feeling in the pit of my stomach.

"Harper!" Blake bellowed as he ran into my bedroom. "What the hell happened?"

He'd obviously heard me, and I knew I'd been screaming loud enough to wake the dead. "I'm sorry. Bad dream," I told him reassuringly. "I'm fine now."

I could see him at the door, the light from the hallway backlighting his state of disarray. With only a pair of flannel pajama pants on,

I could see the ripped muscles of his arms, chest, and stomach. He looked so solid and so strong, yet so endearing. His hair was spiking up in a few places, and he was frowning with concern.

"You sure? You sounded like somebody was killing you."

"Dani," I whispered aloud. "I was dreaming about my sister."

Blake moved into the room and partially closed the door so the light wasn't blinding me. Then he sat down on the bed, propping himself up against the headboard, and pulled my upper body against his.

I took the comforting embrace and laid my head on his shoulder, feeling the scorching heat of his skin against my cheek. "I'm sorry."

"Don't," he answered huskily. "I want to be here for you. I know you're scared. Hell, you'd have to be crazy *not* to be."

After seeing Dani's video, I was downright terrified she was going to die. With the government at a standstill about what they could do and the kidnappers obviously getting restless, I was pretty sure my sister didn't have a lot of time.

Blake and I had eaten early, and then I'd worked on some drawings while he'd tackled some paperwork. The evening had passed pleasantly, but our attraction and chemistry was always there, always present. Blake was like a big magnet that made me want to latch onto him so desperately, like I was ferromagnetic.

I'd finally had to go to bed before I'd done something stupid. All I wanted was to be naked and sweaty with this gorgeous man who was rubbing my back in comfort. And it wasn't because I was emotional or tired.

I wanted Blake Colter, and although I hadn't consciously recognized it, I'd missed him for a dozen or so years.

My heart clenched as he ran a sympathetic hand over my hair, his tenderness making it even harder to push him away.

I was raw, and Blake was the only one who could take away the pain right now.

Not only was I afraid for my sister, but I was trying to deal with the volatile emotions that Blake made me feel.

I sighed, then wondered how he'd managed to get away from all the women who probably threw themselves in his direction. Blake was so addictive that I already wondered how I'd leave him after all this was over. Not only was he hot and sexy, but he was also brilliant and kind. He was the type of guy every woman dreamed about but very seldom discovered. I know that nobody like him had ever crossed my path again.

"Better?" he asked in a guttural tone.

"Yes."

"Then I think I'd better get the hell out of here before I do something we might both regret," he suggested in a pained voice.

"I would never regret it," I encouraged.

"I might," he answered.

"We're adults, Blake. We aren't kids anymore." I'd gladly handle the heat.

I felt his body tense and the room was silent as he threaded his fingers into my hair and fisted it. "Christ, Harper. You have no idea how hard this is for me."

I had an inkling, and as I let my hand trail down his powerful chest and six-pack abs, I traced each muscle before I went lower to stroke over the flannel to appease one very hard cock.

He hissed his approval, then put his hand over mine, as though he was afraid I'd take it away. "Touch me, dammit. Do it."

His command was loud, vocal, and infused with a depth of need that moved me into action. I moved my hand beneath the elastic waist of the loose pants and wrapped my fingers around his shaft. It was smooth and so silky that I stroked him, reveling in the texture of velvety skin over the hardness.

"You feel so good, Blake," I told him in a sultry, needy voice that I barely recognized as my own.

He took control, and before I knew what was happening, I was beneath him and his large hands were pinning my hands over my head.

"I can't do this anymore, Harper. I can't fight with this, with the way that I want you," he growled.

"Then don't," I advised. "Please don't." I wanted this, wanted him.

"I'm not," he answered harshly as he sat me up and pulled the cotton nightgown I was wearing over my head, and then tossed it to the bedroom floor. "I can't. I need you too damn much."

I shuddered as he wrapped his arms around me again, this time skin-to-skin, my hard nipples abrading against his chest.

There was no hesitation as he swooped down and kissed me, devouring my mouth like he was desperate for sustenance. I opened for him, then let our tongues entwine, letting him know I needed this as much as he did.

Maybe more.

I was panting as his mouth finally left mine and his wicked tongue traveled down my neck.

"Blake," I said on a sigh.

He nipped at my skin, and then soothed over it with his tongue. "It's so fucking good to hear *my* name coming from *your* mouth," he answered in a low, muffled voice against my neck.

I realized how few times I'd ever said his name. "I know exactly who you are now," I answered in an aroused voice. "Blake."

"Damn straight," he answered. "The man who is about to make you come so hard you'll be screaming my name by the time we're done."

I shuddered with excitement. "Make me," I challenged.

"Baby, I plan on it."

He let go of my wrists to move his mouth downward, and I speared my hands into his hair, savoring the feel of the coarse locks between my fingers. "Yes."

This didn't feel like the first time, but I didn't want it to. We were all grown up, and Blake was kind, but he was also a dominant male, something that unbelievably turned me on.

I squirmed as his teeth and mouth clamped over one of my sensitive nipples, suckling hard before he used his tongue to lighten the touch.

My back arched, and my body jerked every time he switched from one breast to the other, making the pleasure/pain sensation so arousing that I was about to lose my mind.

"Please," I begged, feeling the pressure building. "I need to come."

"You will. When you're ready," he demanded.

"I'm ready," I whimpered as his fingers probed the delicate silk of my panties.

"Not yet," he denied.

Blake yanked the silk hard, and it gave for him. He quickly disposed of the ruined underwear by flinging it to the floor.

I tossed my head as his mouth continued to tease my nipples, and his fingers invaded my needy pussy.

"Blake. Please," I cried out, desperate for him.

"I've wanted this for years, sweetheart. I'm not going to screw it up."

There wasn't a damn thing he could do wrong. Not while he was touching me. His hands and mouth felt like liquid fire, and I was definitely combustible.

"Fuck me," I pleaded. "I can't play anymore."

"I'm not messing around," he rasped. "Everything about this moment is dead serious."

His thumb circled my clit, and then stroked hard over the bundle of nerves, setting off a series of moans I didn't even try to control.

I raised my hips, trying desperately to get more friction, more pressure. But he backed off, teasing me until I was nearly insane. "Now," I demanded.

He moved between my thighs, then bent my legs up and pushed them apart impatiently. "I haven't tasted you in years. And you're so damn sweet," he rumbled right before he lowered his head and ran his tongue along my slit.

I would have come off the bed if Blake hadn't had a good grasp on me. "More. More." I couldn't handle the teasing another second.

He gave me what I was asking for, delving his tongue between my folds, searching and finding my clit. But he didn't give me quite enough, and I knew it was deliberate. "That feels so amazing."

My body was burning out of control, and I panted as Blake's teeth lightly bit on my clit, then followed it with an intense stroke of his tongue.

Urgently, I fisted his hair, and then pushed his face against my pussy, begging without words for what I needed to come apart.

His tongue was like silk as it licked from bottom to the top of my pink, quivering flesh. He wasn't taking my direction. He had his own agenda, and it was one that I wasn't sure I could handle.

Blake as a young man was kind and insistent.

Blake as a full grown man was hungry, dominant, and in control.

"Oh, God. I can't take anymore," I said breathlessly.

"Yes, you can," he answered in a muffled voice, his mouth full of my quivering flesh.

My legs began to tremble and the knot in my belly started to unfurl as Blake stroked my clit over and over with his tongue, finally giving me what I needed.

"Yes. Yes. Yes."

I chanted my mantra as his greedy tongue kept invading and conquering, leaving me shaking as my climax finally rocked my body. I rode the wave as Blake kept up his rampant, demanding strokes on my clit, licking every drop of juice from my pussy as I imploded.

He came over me quickly, supporting his weight with his hands as he kissed me like a madman, his tongue delving deep into my mouth, letting me taste the flavor of myself in his kiss.

It only enflamed me more.

My body was still trembling, and I needed him inside me.

I didn't have to ask. Blake was obviously not going to wait, and he filled me with one powerful thrust of his hips, groaning as he buried himself to his balls and tore his mouth from mine. "Harper!"

My heart was galloping as he said my name like he was coming home to me. In so many ways, it felt just like that. It felt like we were finally where we were supposed to be.

"Blake!" I cried out, loving the sound of his name.

I lifted my legs around his waist, trying to pull him as close to me as I could possibly get. I welcomed his weight as he lowered himself down onto his elbows and kissed me as he pumped his hips, his cock stretching my internal muscles. It hurt so damn good.

"Blake. Blake. Blake."

I screamed his name with every thrust of his cock. My arms went around his neck, and he kissed me over and over, nibbling at my lips, my neck, then rested his mouth against my temple as he muttered, "Mine. You're mine, Harper. You've always been mine."

"Yes," I agreed with satisfaction, my nails digging into his back as I felt the pleasure of his possession rising to a crescendo of need. "I need you, Blake. I need you."

He increased his pace, pummeling into me as he bit down lightly on my shoulder, and then said, "You have me, sweetheart. You've always had me."

His words made me grip him harder, tighter, my fingers clawing at his skin. My back arched up and my legs tightened around his waist as my orgasm hit hard and frenzied. "Blake!"

I was still screaming, but I didn't care. My body was going up in flames and I was burning in Blake's heat, his frantic pace as he kept slamming into me like a man possessed.

My nails dug into his skin hard, the pleasure of my impending climax so intense that I felt like I was going to shatter.

Blake rose up, grasped my hips, and then pulled them against him as he struggled to get deeper, harder thrusts.

I broke apart, pieces of me flying into the air as I screamed out his name over and over again, the pulsing of my body clamping down on his cock.

"Harper," he groaned huskily. "You feel so damn good, baby."

My channel milked him hard, and his hot release flooded inside me as I shuddered with pure, unadulterated bliss as I watched him lose control.

Blake buried his face against my neck, and I savored the hot spurts of air against my skin as he tried to recover his breathing.

My heart was still thundering, and I was still panting as I fisted his hair as he lowered his mouth to kiss me.

He rolled with our mouths and bodies still joined, letting me sprawl across his hard body as he completed the sensual embrace.

The room was silent. The only sound that could be heard was our harsh breathing.

My body was sated and content as I draped over him like a blanket.

He kissed my temple lightly, and then stated, "Please tell me you're on birth control. I fucked up."

I tensed, just now realizing that he hadn't used a condom.

"I'm not," I said flatly, then pushed on his chest so I could sit up.

Chapter 14

Harper

"I wasn't thinking straight, Harper. It's not your fault. I messed up," he said gruffly as he pulled himself up to sit against the headboard.

The sight of his nude body lounging against the back of the bed momentarily caught me off-guard, and I had to avert my eyes away from him to get my thoughts straight.

I pulled the covers over my own body as I sat cross-legged in the middle of the bed.

"It's not just your responsibility," I mumbled. "I'm not worried. The chances of me getting pregnant right now are pretty slim."

"Why?"

"Wrong time," I told him.

"Well, you definitely don't have to worry about whether or not I'm clean. The last woman I was with was a virgin, and I haven't fucked another woman since then."

My head jerked up, and I knew I was gaping at him like an idiot, but I couldn't imagine… "Me?" I squeaked.

"Yeah. Twelve years ago."

I shook my head. It wasn't possible that a virile guy like Blake hadn't been with anybody since he was in college, since he'd been with me. "How is that possible?" I asked in a confused tone.

"It's pretty simple. I didn't want anyone else."

He absolutely meant he hadn't slept with another female since our youthful encounter, but I still didn't get it. "Why?"

He shrugged. "I used all kinds of excuses to try to convince myself why I wasn't screwing other women after I'd been with you, but they were all bullshit. The real truth is pretty simple. I guess I really was waiting for you. The interest just wasn't there."

"Twelve years with no sex?" I asked incredulously.

"Hell, you make it sound like a crime," he rumbled.

"No. Not a crime. It's just pretty unbelievable."

"Believe it," he said drily. "It's been a very long dry spell."

"Why me?" I asked.

"Because you're the only one I wanted after we were together, Harper. Believe it or not."

"I believe you," I whispered. "I'm just…shocked."

"Because you always thought I slept with a different woman every week?"

I pushed the hair back from my face, knowing I was a sweaty mess. "I thought you were Marcus, and he's definitely no angel."

"I'm no angel, either. In my fantasies, we've done some pretty kinky stuff," he teased.

"In mine, too," I answered.

"Why is it so strange that I haven't been with another woman? I did tell you that night was special to me. I didn't want to tarnish it by being with someone who didn't make me feel the same way," he admitted in a low, hesitant tone. "Have you been with so many men since you lost your virginity that you think it's weird or something?"

I didn't think it was weird. I thought it was probably the most touching, wonderful thing a man could ever say. Not that most guys would admit it. But for a man as hot and virile as Blake to not have touched another woman since me was pretty damn amazing.

I shook my head. "No. I haven't been with anyone else. It's always just been you. Maybe that's why I'm so surprised, and I think it's so special that you haven't, either."

"That's probably why I didn't even think about a condom. I haven't worried about that in years," he said in a remorseful tone. "But I should have."

"I won't get pregnant, Blake," I reassured him.

"If you do, you're going to marry me, dammit," he demanded.

"I wouldn't marry you because of that," I refused. "That's no reason to marry a guy."

"The hell it isn't," he said testily and crossed his arms over his massive chest.

I could see a stubborn streak in him that I'd never noticed before, and I had to bite my lip to keep from smiling.

We didn't have cause to argue about this subject.

Number one—I wasn't going to get pregnant.

Number two—I couldn't possibly marry him.

"I won't get pregnant," I promised him.

"We'll see," Blake said dangerously as he rose from the bed. "I'll let you sleep. You can use the rest."

His words were stiff and cold, like he'd suddenly lost interest in the entire subject.

I suddenly felt cold and lonely, and I wondered what I'd done to make him suddenly shut down. He'd made himself vulnerable to me, and I'd done the same by telling him I'd never been with anybody else.

The only other thing I'd said was that being pregnant was no reason for a man and a woman to marry, which was true. In my case, I had my own means, and I could raise a child just fine by myself. If the alternative was marrying somebody just because I was pregnant, hypothetically, I'd rather go it alone.

He stopped at the door, and then pulled it completely open, flooding the room with bright light. "Just for the record," he said grimly. "If you are pregnant, you *are* going to marry me, Harper. So I suggest you get used to the idea, even if you don't want me for a husband."

He closed the door behind him before I could open my mouth to explain that it wasn't *him* I didn't want. It was him under those circumstances.

For God's sake, I was thirty years old. I had my own money and a career that would allow me to settle down in one place if that's what I wanted. I wouldn't marry unless I really wanted to get married, which would never happen, no matter how much I cared about Blake. In fact, I cared too much about him to make him commit to me. I could never give him everything he wanted. It wasn't possible.

Blake is a US senator. He's a government official, a public figure.

I frowned into the darkness as I slid under the covers and rested my head on a pillow that still smelled like Blake, a masculine, tantalizing scent that instantly made my chest ache.

Was he afraid that having an illegitimate child would ruin his career? I guess the thought had never occurred to me, but I suppose it wouldn't exactly be good in the eyes of the general public.

It could ruin his public image, thus his career in the Senate.

I pulled the sheet and blankets around my nude body, missing Blake's heat.

It seemed so damn backward that any voter would judge Blake by his marital status if he got a woman pregnant. But situations got twisted and ugly in the political news, to the point where people no longer knew what was the truth and what was a lie.

I wanted to tell him the whole truth, the reason why I'd never marry, but I hadn't. I was still reeling from the fact that he'd never slept with another woman in all the years we'd been apart.

He doesn't really want to marry me. He's just readying himself for the possibility of me getting pregnant.

"If that's true, then why hadn't he found somebody to love?" I whispered into the dark, but no answer came back to me.

Chapter 15

Blake

I was still staring at the ceiling when the sun came up, still counting the little textures in the bedroom ceiling with the lights on.

All I fucking knew right now was that I needed Harper. The gnawing ache in my gut wouldn't subside.

I wouldn't marry you for that reason!

I could still hear those words coming out of her beautiful mouth, but I couldn't digest them. Furthermore, I wasn't willing to accept them.

If she wouldn't marry me if she was pregnant, there was probably no chance in the world that she'd marry me at all. For any reason.

Maybe I shouldn't have left. Maybe I should have just fucked her into submission, made her want me just as damn badly as I wanted her. Maybe then she'd be addicted. Hell, I wanted this constant craving to be mutual, even if it was pretty damn miserable right now.

I might have left pissed off, but I sure as hell wasn't giving up. There was no way I could feel like this alone.

My cell phone buzzed on the bedside table and I quickly took a look at the time. It was early, way earlier than anybody would call unless it was pretty damn important.

I snatched the phone, but there was nothing except the number on the caller ID. "Colter," I answered abruptly.

"Yeah, this is Colter, too," Marcus's amused voice answered.

I sat up in bed, wide awake at the sound of my twin's voice.

"Christ! Are you okay? What about Tate?" Truth be told, I'd been confident in Marcus's skills, but I'd been pretty damn worried about both of my brothers.

"We're both fine. We just got to Istanbul. Danica needs medical treatment. She's got some infected wounds, and is so fucking dehydrated that they're pumping her with fluids."

"How bad?" I asked abruptly.

"She'll live. She hates me just as much as ever," Marcus replied drily.

"You didn't tell her the truth?"

"Not yet. Right now she needs to heal. She has a few broken ribs, and she's in a lot of pain. They're better off keeping her medicated and letting her heal. It keeps me from being her target, so I'm good with it, too."

"How long do you think she'll be in the hospital?" I asked, knowing Harper was going to want to see her sister…or at least talk to her.

"If it was up to her, she'd be out already. But I'd say we can keep her in for another couple of days."

"We saw a video," I explained. "She was beat up."

"I saw it," Marcus said abruptly. "She looks worse. Some of the cuts got infected. But tell Harper she'll heal. She's getting good care, and she's stubborn as all hell. Her condition is stable."

I breathed out a sigh of relief. "Harper is going to want to get there."

"Don't," Marcus said abruptly. "I'm getting Danica out of here as soon as she's well enough to make the trip. They're going to want her in DC. I'll fly her there. Tate and I are staying with her until we get her there, so she's safe."

"Think she'll be up to talking?"

"I'll have her call Harper as soon as she's able. I promise. Just let her know she's safe."

"I assume I can be myself now?"

"Yeah. Although it's probably more fun being me than sitting in some uptight Senate gathering in the middle of DC bullshit," he answered good-naturedly.

"Not once in my entire adult life have I ever wanted to be you," I shot back at him.

"Because I'm an asshole," Marcus finished. "Sometimes I don't want to be me, either."

It was a cryptic statement, and I wasn't certain he was completely joking. "I owe you," I answered in a sincere voice. Marcus had saved Danica's life. Judging by her condition, she wouldn't have lasted much longer with her captives.

"You've saved my ass more than once," Marcus reminded me. "Let's call it even."

"So is the team back together again?"

"Hell, no. My sister-in-law would probably shoot me herself if I ever take her husband into dangerous territory again. He's had enough of that shit."

I smiled, imagining Lara, a former FBI agent, threatening to take out Marcus if he ever asked Tate to do another mission. I had no doubt my younger brother would be tempted because he thrived on the adrenaline since he was ex-Special Forces. But I imagined that Lara wouldn't be very keen on Tate running regular assignments. And my younger brother seemed pretty damn content with his current situation. "She just might shoot you," I mused.

"The old team is done. And the new one was thrown together for this operation only. I'm already going to be in hot water with the government since it was unauthorized and everyone will know who was responsible."

"I'll talk to them," I told him gruffly.

As a senator, I had more pull and more friends in high places in DC than Marcus did.

"Do what you can," he answered nonchalantly. "I'm not particularly worried about it. I'm not about to speak about this publicly, and nobody else is going to talk either. Those bastards would have let her die in hostile territory, so what are they going to say? Were they ready to turn over the bad guys we have confined?"

"You know they weren't."

"So they can kiss my ass," Marcus answered irritably.

I grinned, noticing that his opinion of the suits in Washington hadn't changed much. "I'm one of those bastards," I reminded him.

"Nah. You're one of the few decent ones."

I chuckled, happy to hear that he sounded just fine. "I'll call Lara, and I'll let Harper know."

"Tate's already on the phone with Lara," Marcus mentioned, sounding disgusted. "The first thing he had to do was call his wife."

I thought that was pretty normal since Tate and Lara were deeply in love with each other, but Marcus made a relationship sound like a deadly disease. "Then I'll just tell Harper."

"We should be back in DC in less than a week, but I'll keep in touch."

"I have to be there in a week anyway," I contemplated. "I can give her a ride there."

"You two straighten your shit out?" my twin asked bluntly.

"Yes and no," I said evasively. "It's been twelve years. Most of it is water that passed under the bridge a hell of a long time ago."

"Bullshit. It never ended. Harper is the reason you don't get laid more often."

Harper was the reason I didn't get laid *at all.* "She doesn't want to go back there again," I explained away. "She's always thought of me as you, and understandably, she didn't like me very much."

"Then change her mind," Marcus challenged. "You know damn well you want to."

"It's not that simple—"

"Yeah. It is," Marcus interrupted. "You take her to bed and make her come until she can't think straight and you keep her that way. I'm pretty sure that's how our siblings ended up married."

"I think it was a little bit more than that," I said unhappily, not really wanting to share that Harper didn't want me for anything other than some physical gratification.

"You can be charming when you want to, bro."

"Give it up, Marcus."

"Not until you do," he said in an annoyingly persistent voice.

There was no way I was totally giving up, but I didn't share my plans with Marcus…probably because I had none yet.

Changing the subject, I told him, "Tell Tate I'm glad you're both safe."

"Will do. I need to get back to the hospital before Danica wakes up and tries to crawl out the window."

I laughed when I imagined Marcus as Dani's guardian. Somehow, I couldn't see Marcus caring enough to keep her from fleeing. "Then just let her go. She won't go far."

"Like hell I will. She's too damn weak to go anywhere. I'm about to tie her to the hospital bed."

I blinked in surprise at the serious tone of his voice. He was truly…annoyed, and maybe just a little bit concerned. I'd never seen him show much emotion unless it involved his family. "Tell me something…?"

"What?" Marcus asked in a clipped tone.

"If Harper hadn't asked you, would you have tried to rescue Dani anyway?"

There was silence on the line, and for a moment I thought we'd lost our connection.

"Marcus?"

"I don't know. Probably," my older brother finally admitted grudgingly. "She's probably the most annoying female I've ever met, but she's pretty damn gutsy."

"You like her," I accused.

"I wouldn't go that far," he grumbled. "I gotta go. I'll have Danica call Harper as soon as she can."

We hung up after a very brief good-bye, and I tossed my phone back on the bedside table.

I debated for a few minutes whether or not I should wake Harper up to tell her about her sister.

No matter how pissed off I might be at the moment, I knew she'd want to know.

I could see the stress and anxiety on her face every single moment of the day, and her exhaustion was evident.

I rolled out of bed, deciding that if it was me, I'd want to know the moment one of my siblings was out of danger.

Once Harper knew, maybe she could get some rest, and her nightmares about her sister would cease.

After that, we're focusing on us.

It was about damn time Harper Lawson and I settled the fact that she was mine, once and for all.

Maybe she didn't want a commitment right now, but I'd waited this long. I could wait a little bit longer.

Chapter 16

Harper

"Harper?"

I was in some kind of twilight sleep when I heard Blake call my name. Not really asleep, but not quite awake, either.

I blinked several times as I opened my eyes just as he took a seat on the other side of the bed.

Bolting upright, I noticed it was daylight, and the look on his face appeared harsh and tense. He was still in the same flannel pajama bottoms, so I assumed he'd just woken up.

"What happened? Is it Dani?"

"Are you fully awake?" he asked.

"Yes," I shot back immediately. "Tell me."

My stomach was tied up in knots, and I moved closer and put a hand on his bare shoulder to assure him I was listening.

"Marcus found her. She's back across the Turkish border in a hospital being treated for dehydration and malnourishment. But she's okay. A few infected wounds, but she's healing."

Relief flooded through my body, and my hand dropped from Blake's arm. "Thank God. Can I see her?" I questioned tearfully.

He shook his head. "By the time you get a visa and make the trip there, Dani should be headed home. Tate and Marcus are staying with her to make sure she doesn't try to escape the hospital, then they're bringing her to Washington so she can undergo some debriefing if she's able. If she needs more medical care, she can get it in Washington. She'll fly in comfort in Marcus's jet."

A startled laugh escaped my mouth, but I knew that given the chance, Dani probably *would* try to get the hell out of the hospital on her own. She'd always hated being fussed over, and she definitely didn't deal very well with being under the weather. When we were kids, just getting her tonsils out had become a major ordeal for my parents.

"Then I can meet her in DC," I decided. "How long will it take for her to get there?"

Blake shrugged. "Probably close to a week, if Marcus can keep her in the hospital for treatment. She was really dehydrated, and Marcus said she's really thin."

"Is she…okay emotionally?" The question came out of my mouth without really knowing what I was asking. All I wanted to know was if she was still the same Dani.

"You want to know if they raped her?"

I slowly nodded. "Yes."

"I'm not sure," Blake admitted. "She was beaten up pretty badly, but if Marcus didn't mention sexual assault, I doubt it. He seemed pretty pissed off about everything they'd done to her, but he didn't mention any kind of sexual offenses."

"She'll recover. She's one of the strongest people I know," I said firmly, refusing to believe that my sister would be anything other than herself again. "She doesn't know about you two—"

"Marcus will tell her when she's strong enough to understand," Blake interrupted. "I doubt he'll continue to let her believe that he's that big of an asshole." He paused before adding, "On second thought, he's not exactly warm and fuzzy, but he isn't the type to deliberately hurt somebody either."

Tears of gratitude began to cascade down my cheeks. "I don't know how I'll ever repay all of you for what you've done. I was so afraid they'd kill her."

"Maybe you can sleep without nightmares, now," he answered hoarsely as he put his hand gently on my face and swiped away my tears with his thumb.

Without another thought, I threw myself in his arms, and he caught my naked body, holding me tightly as I cried.

"Thank you," I whispered into his ear.

I knew that Blake had not only covered for Marcus, but he'd called in as many favors as he possibly could in Washington. No doubt he'd keep doing it because his brothers might find themselves knee-deep in government bullshit since they'd done something completely out of line in another country.

I had no doubt he'd also help my sister smooth out her own situation there, too.

I cried tears of joy that my sister was safe, while I clung to Blake and let myself sink into his warmth.

His arms came more tightly around me, stroking my back while I let out every bit of anxiety and tension I'd had as a constant companion since I'd realized Dani was being held in captivity by a group of rebels who would likely kill her.

"Crying this hard can't be good for you," Blake grumbled as I felt him rest his chin on the top of my head.

I sniffled as my sobs came to a halt. "I don't know, it feels pretty damn good to me," I answered with a watery smile. "I think it's therapeutic."

"Then you can keep on doing it if you want," he relented.

I pulled back and shot him an enormous grin. "Thanks. But I've cried more during the last few weeks than I have in a very long time. I think it's time to be happy that my sister is okay. I just wish I could see her."

Although I believed Blake, I just wanted to see Dani's face.

He nodded sharply. "I know. I wish she had been well enough to fly back immediately. But it's safer this way."

"If she needed medical treatment, my selfish need to hug her can wait," I told him.

"I asked Marcus to have her call you as soon as she was awake and alert enough to have a conversation. She's weak right now."

"I'm sure she needs sleep." I know I sure as hell hadn't slept good since Dani had disappeared. I could only imagine how seldom she actually slept, knowing that she might die at any moment.

He surveyed me carefully before he asked, "You want to do something for me?"

I nodded slowly. Right now I think I'd do anything for the Colters, just to let them know how much I appreciated what they'd done to rescue my sister.

"Spend some time with me," he requested in a husky voice. "Be with me this week, then fly back to DC with me. Dani will just be arriving or nearly ending her journey to get there."

I looked at him in confusion. "Why? That wouldn't be any kind of favor. I've pushed off my Boston job until next week. I have nothing else to do. It's not exactly a sacrifice." I hesitated a moment before asking, "Or are we talking about sex?"

He shook his head. "Sex or no sex. It only happens if you want it to. I just want you to be with me."

I wasn't sure how to handle his request. I didn't understand it. Maybe if he was requesting that I repay him with sex, it might make sense. But that wasn't what he was asking.

"What do you want me to do?"

"Treat me like I'm Blake and not Marcus."

"I already do."

He shook his head. "You've spent years hating Marcus, or a man you thought was him. Get to know *me*, the man you really gave your virginity to. Maybe if you get to know *me*, you won't be so pissed off at me anymore."

I gaped at him, examining the sincerity of his gaze. "I'm not angry anymore, Blake. I'm really not. I don't regret what happened all those years ago now. Neither one of us was really at fault for the misunderstanding."

He grasped my upper arms lightly. "Then show me. Let this whole thing end with us feeling the way we did twelve years ago."

My tongue darted out to lick my dry lips as I wondered if Blake and I could ever just be friends. The thought of never seeing him again after I left Washington was so painful that my heart already ached. On my side, staying friends would be difficult because I'd always want more, things I couldn't have. "I'll never stop seeing you as the only man who can make me come like I never imagined I could," I told him bluntly.

A slow grin formed on his face. "I'd be glad to oblige you again anytime you want."

My heart flip-flopped as I saw the invitation in his eyes, and it made me want to straddle him and ride him until my aching heart was satisfied. But that would only be a temporary solution.

As though he could hear my thoughts, Blake ordered, "Don't think, Harper. Just feel and enjoy yourself. Be exactly who you are."

"If I'm going to act on my natural instincts, I'd need you naked," I said honestly. "Then I'd need you to let me ride you until I couldn't do anything but scream your name. And you'd have to let me have my way with you first. That's exactly what I'm thinking right now."

His eyes flared with molten heat, and he stared at me with an intensity I couldn't name as he stood up and slipped off his pajama bottoms, liberating a cock that was hard and swollen.

Blake didn't seem to have any inhibitions about being naked. Of course, with a body like his, I don't think anybody as built as Blake would really care.

"I thought you'd never ask," he said gutturally as he laid down on the top of the covers. "I'm all yours."

My core clenched, and my heart swelled as I looked at Blake making himself vulnerable and naked—quite literally—to me.

"I need to touch you," I told him nervously.

"Then, for God's sake, do it. If you don't put your hands and those beautiful lips on my body now, I'll have you under me in five seconds. I won't be able to hold myself back," he growled.

I smiled and moved in closer, my hands trembling as I finally got to touch him exactly the way I'd wanted to for so many years that every need I'd bottled up inside me exploded once my palms landed on his chest, and the cork to the bottle holding my emotions back finally *popped.*

Chapter 17

Harper

I was a worrier by nature, a perfectionist who punished herself if everything wasn't just right. But the moment my hands landed on Blake's ripped, perfect body, every thought that I had, anything that I fretted about, flew from my mind.

My only thought was about the pleasure of touching his hot, hard body until I was satisfied. Until *he* was the one calling out *my* name, begging for mercy.

Granted, I didn't have much experience with that kind of thing. But with Blake, I was pretty sure all I had to do was please *myself* to please *him*.

I moved my hands down his chest, tracing every well delineated muscle in his abdomen, and then bending to run my tongue over the same lines, savoring the salty taste of his skin.

"Harper," he said in a tone that sounded very much like an agonized warning.

I knew where he wanted my touch, and I finally gave it to him as my mouth moved lower, the masculine scent of him nearly making me crazy as I gently wrapped my hand around his engorged cock.

"Do you remember when I told you that your dick was too big?" I asked in an awed voice.

"Yeah." There was a trace of humor in his husky tone.

"I take it back. You're perfect, Blake."

And he *was* absolutely splendid, the velvety shaft so hard it was almost pulsating in my grip.

His body visibly tensed as I toyed with him, fascinated by some of the little things about his manhood that I should have experienced way before the age of thirty.

As I stroked a finger over his balls, he finally reached down and grasped my wrist. "Don't. I'm not sure how much more I can take."

"I thought you said you were all mine," I said with mock innocence. There was nothing that turned me on more than knowing Blake was close to losing it.

"I am," he answered gruffly. "But I'm no use to you if I come and my dick goes limp."

He was wrong. So very wrong. Blake was worth everything to me, whether he could get it up or not. Pleasing him was my secret desire, whether he was inside me or not.

Ignoring his protest, I broke away from his hold, and then bent my head down to taste him, going with my instincts now. He was going to belong to me right now, and I was going to grasp the opportunity to savor him, just like he'd done to me.

His big body shuddered as my tongue circled the soft head, licking off the drop of moisture beaded at the very tip. He tasted masculine and strong, tangy and addictive. "Mmm," I hummed and then opened my mouth to suck in as much of his cock as I possibly could.

"Christ, Harper. This is better than my goddamn fantasies," he groaned, then threaded his hands through my hair. "Baby, you don't have to do this."

I sucked on him like he was my own personal lollipop, letting him slide out of my mouth for a moment as I answered, "Yes. I do. I want it."

"Fuck! Then by all means continue," he rasped greedily.

I took my time, savoring every groan that left Blake's lips, every buck of his hips, and his hands fisting in my hair to guide me up and down his cock. When I finally caught his rhythm, I let my slick fingers follow my mouth so I could enfold his entire length with my fist and my mouth.

I felt totally immersed in him. We started moving in sync, and the feral sounds leaving his mouth mesmerized me.

I didn't care if I was doing things right.

All I wanted was to pleasure him.

"Harper! Not like this. Not this time," he barked as he sat straight up. I would have reared back if he hadn't grabbed me and pulled me on top of his body to straddle him.

"Blake, I wanted—"

"I wanted it, too. But I want to be inside you more," he said in a graveled voice as he eased back down and grabbed my ass, pulling me on top of his erection.

My sheath clenched from his words, the channel suddenly feeling empty. I needed him so desperately that I knew I either had to have him or die of a longing I couldn't remember experiencing before.

Not even the first time, when he'd initiated me to sex.

"Condom in the pocket of my pajama pants," he said in a raspy tone.

I bent as far over on the bed as possible, slipping halfway off his body as I fumbled with his flannel pants until I pulled out the condom.

I was back on him in moments, ripping open the package and slowly slipping it on with a little guidance from him.

I fisted him and then slid on top of his cock, coating the tip with my own juices. Then, I moved down slowly, not quite sure what I was doing, but following my instincts again.

My body was begging me to let him fill me.

And I listened.

"Yesssss," I hissed in pleasure as I sunk down on his shaft, feeling Blake's cock stretching me to capacity.

"Harper. Holy hell. You're fucking destroying me," Blake mumbled as he gripped my hips.

"Is that good?" I asked hesitantly.

"Good and bad. But right now I don't give a fuck. Just ride me," he demanded.

I fell forward and braced my hands beside his head, needing to kiss him, meet our lips like we'd just joined our bodies.

I wanted to drown in him, to be so connected that we'd never be separated again.

I lowered my head, and Blake grasped my hair and jerked me down, his desperation almost palpable as he held my head in place, devouring my mouth boldly, almost violently as he thrust his tongue into my mouth like he wanted to claim me. It was exactly what I longed to have. I wanted him just as needy as I was—out of control and reckless.

I was breathless when he finally released my hair and allowed me to breathe again. I began to sit up, but Blake put a hand to my back. "Stay. I want to feel all of you right now, Harper."

His tone was so sincere, so sexy and aroused that I relaxed on top of him, burying my face in his neck.

Blake guided my hips slowly at first, thrusting up into me harder and harder as his pace quickened. I picked up the motions, and I lowered myself down as he lunged up, our bodies meeting with a slap of skin on every stroke.

I whimpered into his neck, my body igniting as he started to grind against my clit with every hard plunge.

"Jesus, Harper. I feel like I've waited forever for this, for you," Blake said, his voice harsh.

I knew exactly what he meant. I think so much of me had been waiting for him, too. I know my body had yearned for him, and it had been anticipating his return for twelve long years.

Even if there was no chance for us, it didn't keep me from craving him.

"Blake!" I cried out as I felt my climax building, coming close to release.

"Come for me, sweet Harper," he commanded. "Let go."

He started pounding into me hard and deep, seeming to relish and savor every thrust.

I bit his neck lightly as my orgasm consumed me, needing to keep connecting us somehow. Then I traced my tongue along the pulse in his neck as my body began to shudder in release.

Holding my ass exactly where he wanted it, Blake pushed upward a few more times, burying himself hot and hard inside me to the root.

His back arched and his head fell back onto the pillow as he found his own heated release.

And as long as I lived, I knew I'd never forget how erotically beautiful he looked right at that moment.

We laid there together, both of us unable to speak as we panted for breath.

I had to bite my tongue to stop myself from telling him exactly how I felt while he held me on top of his body, unwilling to let me go while our heartbeats slowed back to a normal cadence.

I wanted to tell him that I felt wonderful.

I wanted to tell him that what had just happened was magic.

But mostly, I wanted to tell him I felt…loved.

In the end, I didn't say anything because I knew this was just stolen time. I hugged him to me and left the words unspoken.

Chapter 18

Harper

I heard from Dani the next day. She called while I was fixing breakfast and Blake was upstairs getting into the shower.

I quickly turned down the food on the stove and dove for my cell phone on the counter, hoping it was my sister, and I'd finally be able to hear her voice.

I fumbled to answer the call, nearly breathless as I answered, "Hello."

"Hey big sister," Dani said in a casual voice. "You sound like you just went out for a run."

"Oh, my God. Dani? Please tell me you're okay," I begged.

"I'm okay, Harper. Stop worrying."

"Stop worrying?" I squeaked. "You were kidnapped by a bunch of terrorists, and you want me to stop worrying? Even Mason, Jett, and Carter have been worried sick."

My three brothers seldom lost their cool about anything, so the outright fear they'd been showing since Dani's kidnapping was highly unusual.

"I'm doing good. I just want to get the hell out of here," she complained.

"When are you getting out of the hospital?" I asked anxiously.

"As soon as Marcus the Prick thinks I'm well enough to make the trip back home," Dani said in a hostile tone. "He's such a control freak."

"He rescued *you*," I reminded her.

"He cheated on *you*," she retorted.

"Dani, didn't he tell you?" Marcus had been in Dani's company way long enough to have told her about the mix-up.

"Tell me what?"

She sounded so confused that I quickly related what had happened, and the truth about Blake being the actual brother I'd slept with.

"So nobody cheated on anybody," I finished.

Dani sighed into the phone. "Okay. So I guess he's innocent of taking my sister's virginity and then screwing another woman right after he did it. But he's still an asshole. He orders me around like he's my damn boss."

"I have to admit he's a little…intense," I admitted.

"Intense? I've never even seen the guy crack a smile. And he acts like a damn dictator."

I smiled because Dani's temper could be pretty fierce when she was pissed off. "Give him a break. He did risk his life to save you."

"Yeah. And he never lets me forget about that for even a second," she answered drily.

I leaned my hip against the counter, smiling broader as I imagined throwing Marcus and Dani together. Knowing my little sister as well as I did, and having now met Marcus, I decided they definitely wouldn't play nice with each other. "I was planning on meeting you in DC when you came back."

"Don't!" she answered in a rush. "I'll only be there for one day. I'd rather come see you in Boston. Marcus said you'd be headed there soon."

"Why do I have a feeling you want to get away from Marcus?" I teased, assuming that Marcus had picked up the information about me heading to Boston at the family dinner, when I'd been talking about it with Aileen.

"Probably because I *do* want to get away from him. Desperately."

"How is Tate?" I asked, trying to steer Dani away from talking about Marcus.

"He's cool," she replied, her voice a little lighter. "Unfortunately, he agrees with Marcus on almost everything."

I let out an exasperated sigh. "Dani, you were kidnapped, confined, starved, and abused. There's no way you can possibly be *fine* after an experience like that. Give them and yourself a little slack."

"I never said I was fine," she replied in a quiet voice. "But I'm okay."

"How bad was it?"

"I'll talk to you about it sometime after I get back to the States. Not now, okay?"

I sensed there were things she wasn't quite ready to discuss. "I'm just glad you're safe. I love you."

"I love you, too, sis," she answered in a more emotional voice. "So tell me where you'll be in Boston."

We chatted for a while longer, and I gave her the information for my temporary lodgings in Massachusetts.

"Are you sure you don't want me to come to DC?" I asked her.

"Absolutely not. I'll answer the questions the feds have, and then I'm out of there." She hesitated before she queried, "How were things with the senator? I can't believe we thought your first love was always Marcus."

"I wouldn't say he was exactly my first love. It was one night."

"Come on, Harper. I was there, remember? I saw the broken-up look on your face when you saw Marcus with another woman. Okay. Yeah. It wasn't the guy you had actually slept with, but I could see the pain in your eyes because you thought he was. He was more than just some guy you could tolerate sleeping with. And I know how much it hurt later. This is me, your sister who knows everything about you."

"It was a crush," I insisted.

"Yeah. Whatever. Call it what you want, but he meant something to you."

"He meant a lot," I finally admitted. "But it's been years. He's a nice man, and I'm grateful that I know that now."

"Did you do him?" Dani asked bluntly.

"I'd say that's none of your business," I chastised her.

"Aha! So you did," she answered perceptively. "I can tell by your uptight answer."

"I'm not having this conversation," I warned her.

"We don't have to. I can tell by the sound of your voice that it happened again. But that's not a bad thing, right? I mean, you're older and wiser. You know he's a good guy. It could work."

"I'm an architect who travels around the globe doing historic jobs. Blake is a US senator who travels between Colorado and DC. It would be impossible to have a relationship, even if we wanted it. But we don't."

"*You* don't or *he* doesn't?"

I sighed. "Neither one of us meant for anything to happen. I don't regret it, but Blake wasn't looking for something permanent, and I wasn't, either. You know my situation. I can't do anything long term."

"Sometimes you just have to figure things out," Dani observed thoughtfully.

"We have figured it out. I go to my job in Boston, and he goes back to Congress," I said defensively. Blake had never talked about the future, and the last thing I wanted was to be brokenhearted over the same guy…again. But considering how I felt about him, it was going to be impossible to escape the pain when I left.

"We'll see," Dani said with humor in her voice.

"Take care of yourself, and don't push yourself to feel normal right away. It sounds like you need to regain weight and your strength."

"Oh, God. Now you sound like Marcus."

I rolled my eyes. "I sound like your older sister who loves you."

"Sorry. I know. It's just—I really need some space from all of this."

I was pretty sure she needed a lot of things, and I wanted to reach right through the phone and hug her. "I'll see you in Boston Friday night."

"I'll be there. I wish I could get the hell out of here earlier, but I swear, Marcus and Tate are everywhere."

"Then be patient," I advised. "It's only for a few more days."

Dani grumbled, never promising she wouldn't at least try to escape, but I was pretty confident that Marcus and Tate weren't going to let her go anywhere.

Before she hung up, I had to ask, "Why exactly did you cross that border? Are the rumors about you helping those kids true?"

Dani was silent for a moment before she confessed, "The reports are pretty accurate, but that doesn't make me some kind of hero. What adult could let those kids end up dead?"

I wanted to tell her probably plenty of them if it meant they might very well die for helping those teenagers. She'd known she was going to get caught, yet she'd surrendered herself to save a few kids. Dani had to have been terrified, yet she'd done it.

"Come home safe," I said in a pleading voice.

"I will. I promise. We'll hang out together in Boston for a while. I doubt my boss is going to let me go back on assignment anytime soon, especially since the incident went public."

We said our good-byes and hung up. I put my phone down on the counter and went to stir the pots that were still warming on the stove, dreading the moment when I'd actually have to tell Blake good-bye.

Harper

"You look pretty damn sexy when you're concentrating," Blake said mischievously from his seat behind the desk of his home office.

I looked up and met his gaze, and then started to squirm on the couch across the room from him.

Neither one of us had ever said another word about Blake's plan to get to know each other again…or maybe it was for the first time since we didn't talk much twelve years ago. It had just…happened. Since I'd gotten the chance to talk to Dani yesterday, my heart was considerably lighter.

Both yesterday and today, Blake had taken me around his research ranch, showing me how he was developing healthier breeds of cattle. I'd met some of his employees, other researchers who continued development while Blake was away.

We visited his pregnant heifers, and I got to get up close and personal with some pretty cranky bulls. Luckily, there had been a fence between me and the ornery males, and that was really as close as I wanted to get.

It was an amazing place, and I could tell Blake loved what he was doing. Some of the information on DNA and genetics went a bit above my head, but Blake was always happy to explain.

Finally, after we'd exchanged a couple of heart-pounding glances, I answered, "I look like a woman who barely got to shower this morning, all because a wildman decided he liked morning sex-capades, then didn't give me time to put on any makeup before he dragged me away from the house. I'm far from beautiful," I told him.

If the truth be told, I was a mess. I hadn't changed out of my jeans and long-sleeved shirt I'd worn to walk around the ranch with him, and I was sitting in the middle of his office couch with my hair half down and half up, trying to work on my design concept for the new office buildings in Boston. With a large sketchbook in my hand, I'd been drawing when he'd thrown out his compliment, one of many over the last few days that had me wondering if he was blind.

"I think showering together is the best way I've ever discovered to get rid of my morning wood," he answered with a grin.

I rolled my eyes. "Do you ever stop thinking about sex?"

Yeah, that was probably an unfair question since I never seemed to think about anything else when we were together. Even after a day of hiking around his ranch in a worn-out sweatshirt and a pair of jeans, Blake was the hottest guy I'd ever seen.

"No," he admitted. "I'm pretty much always thinking about sex when you're sitting in the same room with me."

"Should I go?" I asked, already knowing he'd refuse. Blake had been the one who suggested we work together in his office.

"Hell, no. And deprive me of the opportunity to torture myself? Not happening."

I laughed simply because he was being so ridiculous. Blake had a quirky sense of humor that I understood extremely well.

Letting out a mock sigh, I replied, "That would be a shame. Opportunities to be a masochist don't really come around that often."

"Damned if I do, and damned if I don't," he grumbled as he looked back at his computer.

"What?"

He shot me a befuddled glance. "I don't want you anywhere else but with me, but it's also torture when you are in the room and I'm not fucking you senseless."

I actually giggled before I turned my attention back to my drawings, secretly loving the way that Blake always wanted me near him. It wasn't a suffocating thing. It just felt good to know he wanted my company, and to know he was more comfortable when we were close. I'd never experienced that kind of intimacy with another person before, so I savored the feeling of being wanted.

"Even if you *aren't* fucking me, there's no place I'd rather be," I answered honestly.

"Same here," he answered huskily. "If I can't fuck you, I at least want to be close to you."

My heart squeezed from the emotions that his words suddenly awakened. Blake moved me, even when he was talking dirty.

I'd never really experienced happiness just from being in the same room with another guy, but that was exactly what happened when I was near Blake.

It felt natural, normal.

I'd been alone for so long that I was content in my own company.

But maybe I'd just never realized there was something missing, not until I'd spent time with Blake.

It didn't matter that we were both working. Just being in the same room with him made me aware of how connected we felt sometimes.

However, it was also a distraction, and I couldn't help stealing an occasional glance in his direction just to stare at his powerful, chiseled features, and his cropped but amazingly thick hair that had me itching to go tangle my fingers in the textured strands.

He looked up quickly, catching me watching him, and then grinned as he leaned back in his chair. "You know I'm not getting a damn thing done."

"Sorry," I answered in a quiet tone, and I was so *not* sorry at all. The way that he looked at me made me feel like the most desired woman on Earth. His gray eyes stared so hungrily, so intensely that I was squirming under his stare again.

For just a moment, I allowed myself to pretend that Blake's attention wasn't all about sex and imagined that he cherished me. The look on his face was almost the same expression that I'd seen Gabe Walker shoot at Chloe several times during their family dinner—a glance just to make sure Chloe was still beside him and happy.

He grinned even wider. "I'm not sorry. I'd sure as hell rather be distracted than not have you here at all."

I knew that I'd be headed for Boston soon, and Blake would be off to DC. But I couldn't resist experiencing the full gamut of emotions that this man could wring out of me.

I'd never had this thing between Blake and I happen to me before, and I was pretty sure it might never happen again. I'd finally decided to relax and enjoy it.

I'd certainly felt a connection with him twelve years ago. I wouldn't have given him my virginity if I hadn't. But this was deeper, richer. Maybe I'd needed to grow up to know just how rare it was to feel this way about a guy.

"I have to leave for Boston Friday," I told him with a touch of sadness in my voice.

"It's Tuesday evening. I thought you were going to wait and fly to Washington with me first on Friday."

"Dani asked me not to come there. She's says she's only spending a few hours there, and then she'll meet me in Boston."

"She probably can't wait to get away from Marcus," Blake observed in a surly tone.

"Maybe." Actually, I was certain he was right, but I didn't want to break my sister's confidence.

Blake stood and strode over to the couch, unceremoniously lifting me from the sofa, only to sit back down with me across his lap.

I squealed in surprise, and then clung to his shoulders as he shifted us into a comfortable position.

"I don't like it. That gives me much less time than I thought," he grumbled.

"Time for what?" I looked at him, pretty certain the question was in my eyes.

"For you to understand that what happened between us twelve years ago was special, and that I could never have betrayed you back then," he rasped. "You've spent over a decade hating me. I don't want you to feel that way anymore."

"I don't," I assured him, toying with his hair gently. "And I didn't hate *you*. I hated Marcus." But I had really never hated Blake's twin, either. I'd hated a miscommunication that had happened and a man who had never really existed.

"But you thought I'd used you. Admit it," he cajoled.

"I did. But that's over, Blake. I don't hate you. I never really could, even when I thought you'd completely played me. That night had been too special for me." Sure, I'd wanted to despise him, but before my emotions could get that negative, I'd see the face of the young man who'd been there to comfort me, protect me, sent me into a world of sensual pleasure that I never knew existed, and then had finally taken me home where I'd belonged.

Blake wrapped his arms around my waist. "I always wanted to know how things had turned out, but I'd never wanted to mention that night we spent together to anybody. Did you square things with your parents?"

I nodded. "I did. We talked most of the day and evening. I admitted that I'd been a complete and total self-absorbed bitch. And they wondered if they'd sheltered me way too much."

"What was decided?"

"I decided I loved them both, and they'd always tried to give me everything I wanted. Maybe it was too much and too easy for a young woman to have that much freedom. But it didn't matter. We were close after that. They supported all of my choices, even my decision to go to school in California." I sighed. "In hindsight, I kind of wish I'd stayed local. It just never occurred to me that I'd lose them so young."

Blake stroked a hand over my hair. "Don't, Harper. There was no way you could predict a random accident like that."

"In my rational mind, I realize that. But I can't help occasionally having regrets. I saw them on every vacation I had from school, but

I missed a lot by not being here in Colorado." I took a shaky breath before I added, "I'd like to go visit their graves. I haven't been there since the funeral. I haven't been back here. We were all in so much shock that I'm not even sure exactly where it is."

"I know. I can take you," Blake said gently.

I frowned at him. "But you were away. You weren't at the service."

He shrugged. "But I've visited there since. I've gone with Mom a few times, and I try to go by and leave some flowers when I'm here."

"Why?" I asked, astonished.

He shrugged. "I knew you'd all moved away, and I'd want somebody to do the same for me if I couldn't go myself very often. I go there to talk to my dad sometimes. I'm not sure if he hears me, but I always feel better afterward."

My heart tripped as I looked at his solemn expression. "You were so young when he passed away."

"I still miss him," Blake answered grimly. "I don't think the pain of losing a parent ever goes away. It just gets less acute."

He was right, and my heart ached for the boy Blake had been when his father had been killed in an accident even stranger than the car collision that had killed my parents. "Thank you for visiting the cemetery when we couldn't."

"It's no big deal," he answered nonchalantly, but his arms tightened around my waist.

I laid my hand on his shoulder and wrapped my arms around his neck. He smelled so good, felt so warm and real that I relished the sense of pleasure it gave me just to be close to him.

Blake was probably one of the most complex but kindest men I'd ever met. "My mom loved your mother like a sister," I confided.

"I know. Mom still mourns over losing her best friend," Blake answered.

We were silent as we sat there together, comfortable in each other's arms. It wasn't awkward or difficult. In fact, for the first time since I'd returned to Rocky Springs, I actually felt like I was really home.

Chapter 20

Blake

"Are you glad you don't have to be Marcus anymore?" Harper asked me curiously as we sat in a small Mexican restaurant, having dinner in Rocky Springs the next day.

As promised, we'd visited her parents' resting place in the cemetery, and my father's gravesite. Harper had insisted on getting the flowers for my dad's site in addition to her own for her mom and dad.

She said each flower she picked up had meaning, but all I could remember was her solemn expression as she'd decorated all of the graves with beautiful blooms that would probably die off the next day. It was still cold in the Colorado mountains at night. But Harper hadn't seemed to care. She'd been adamant about leaving every single flower, and I have to admit that my dad's resting place had never looked so nice.

As we stood by each headstone, we'd shared some of our better memories about our parents. Some of the things that came to mind about my dad I hadn't even thought about for years.

I considered her question for a moment before answering, "When we were kids, I *did* want to be Marcus."

Harper looked up from her food and frowned. "Why?"

"He always knew what his future was going to be, and he had balls. I didn't think there was anything he was afraid of, and we were close back then."

"You aren't close now?" Harper asked.

"I'm not sure anybody can really be close to Marcus. He's changed. We used to have the connection that people talk about with identical twins. We could almost sense each other's emotions. But once he started traveling the world, we just drifted apart." I still wasn't sure what had happened. "Since I started helping him cover his disappearances, we've gotten closer, but it's never been the same as it was when we were children."

"We're never as innocent, either," Harper said thoughtfully. "Sometimes as we get older, we want to keep more things to ourselves."

"What are your secrets?" I asked her, because I really wanted to know.

She shrugged. "Some things don't ever need to be told." Then she smiled. "Personally, I'm glad you're not Marcus, and that you don't want to be him anymore. You're wonderful just the way you are."

"If you think that, then I'm glad I don't want to be Marcus, either." As identical twins, maybe my brother and I had both gone through some identity crises when we were young, but we'd grown into two very distinct individuals.

"You found your own place, your own calling," Harper observed.

"It just took me a little longer than Marcus. He always knew he was going to run my father's company. None of the rest of us were even remotely interested in taking it over."

"So you finally figured out you shared Zane's talent for science?" Harper asked as she laid her napkin on her plate, her dinner finished.

"Not as quickly as Zane did. Hell, he was always scientifically gifted, even as a kid."

She took a sip of her wine before she commented, "Sometimes it takes a little longer to figure out where you belong in life."

I knew damn well she was referring to her own late awakening that she wanted to make something out of her life rather than just being a rich man's daughter. "Like you figuring out you wanted to preserve historic buildings while still updating the rest of the facilities?"

She laughed, a genuine sound that made my chest ache. Harper was beautiful when she smiled, her happiness almost infectious. She'd left her gorgeous blonde hair down today, but she was still in jeans and an old college sweatshirt. Casual seemed to be her comfort zone, and it looked damn good on her.

"I always liked old buildings," she explained. "When I chose an architecture major, it was because I'd always been good at creating, visualizing places how I thought they should or could be. The specialty area happened completely by accident, but I love it. I wouldn't want to do anything else."

"You're good at it," I answered honestly. I'd seen photos of some of her projects. She did have amazing vision and talent.

"Thanks," she murmured. "I'd like to think I leave a little part of myself in every job."

I had no doubt that she left a tiny piece of her *soul* in every place she designed. Because that was part of her personality. Everything she did, she seemed to put herself into heart and soul.

Even the simple task of bringing flowers to a gravesite.

Or buying property to build a homeless shelter in cities that desperately needed it.

I remembered how much I wanted to help Harper assist more of the homeless. "I would really like to get your work with the homeless set up as an official charity. Are you sure you're okay with that? I know a lot of people who would be supporters and give donations."

Harper tilted her head, like she was thinking about the implications of her work becoming an official charity. She'd seemed fine with the idea before, but I wanted to make sure she hadn't changed her mind before I started the paperwork.

"I think I'd like to move forward if you think it will help more of the people without a roof over their heads. Right now, I'm just working on temporary shelter, but that's only a small part of a solution. We need long-term housing for these people, mental health workers, and so many more resources than I could ever provide myself."

I could hear the passion in her voice as she started talking about her work with people who needed homes. She was pretty amazing. That single incident twelve years ago had impacted her life so significantly. Only someone with a huge heart would continue to care so damn much. Harper could talk about how spoiled she'd been as a kid, and believe me, I knew it firsthand, but she'd been a product of her isolation from the real world. She'd grown into the most incredible woman I'd ever known.

"I'll handle it," I assured her. And I really wanted to be involved. Harper had started something important, and I wanted to help her make it grow. Maybe one charity couldn't singlehandedly deal with the homeless problem in our country, but we could certainly make a dent in the progress.

She nodded. "What are we doing tomorrow?"

To be honest, I was trying not to think about tomorrow, her last day with me here in Rocky Springs.

"I don't want this to end, Harper. Not on Friday. Why does it have to? I can come to Boston to visit, and you could come to DC. I have a damn private jet at my disposal. We can still see each other." My gut ached already just from the thought of Harper leaving me.

She shook her head slowly. "Long-distance relationships rarely work, Blake. You know that. We both know our lifestyles and personalities aren't conducive to a casual, long-distance arrangement."

The last thing *any* relationship I had with Harper would be was *casual.* I wanted to complicate everything, see her every moment that I had away from work. And that didn't mean once a month, or every few months. I wanted her to be...mine. "It doesn't matter. I still want it. I still want to see you."

Harper was silent as she gazed at me across the table. Finally, she shook her head again. "It won't work for me. I'm sorry. All we could ever be is friends, and I don't think I can do that. I'd want...more."

"Then take more. It's not like I'm not willing to give you whatever you want."

Christ! Did she not get it? I'd waited my entire adult life for her. There had never been anyone but Harper for me, and there never would be. If she left again, I'd be completely useless, fucking destroyed.

Maybe before I'd seen her again, I could put Harper away in a separate compartment and not think about her, but that isn't going to work for me anymore.

I glared at her, watching as she swallowed hard and avoided looking at me directly as she said, "You're not the problem, Blake. It's me. I can never give you what you deserve."

She rose to her feet and started putting on her coat, barely giving me time to pay the check before she walked outside.

I followed, angry that I couldn't figure out what was wrong, why we couldn't make this work. Yeah, maybe it wasn't the best of situations, but when you find the person you want to spend the rest of your life with, compromises could be made.

"Harper!" I grabbed her arm and turned her around to face me as she hurried toward the car. "We can work this out. I know we can."

"We can't," she said stubbornly.

"Why?"

"It's personal, Blake. But believe me, it's all me. You're an incredible guy, and if I was a normal woman, I'd be bending over backward to keep you in my life."

Her emerald eyes were glistening with tears, and it sliced my heart to ribbons to see her this way. Something was tormenting her, and I wanted to know exactly what it was so I could make it go away. "Why aren't you normal?"

There wasn't one damn thing wrong with her. In my eyes, she was perfect.

"Can't you just accept that we'll never have anything beyond the time we've had in the last few weeks?"

"No, goddammit, I can't," I answered harshly. "I can't accept that we're just never going to see each other again. I can't accept that we can't work this out. And I sure as hell can't accept that you don't care about me as much as I care about you."

Her expression grew distant. "You have to. I am leaving and I can't see you again."

"What if you're pregnant?" I asked desperately.

"Let's not think about that. Do you really want to be a father?"

"Hell, yes. Of course I do. If you get pregnant, I'd want us to be together. I want us to be together if you're not pregnant right now."

"I'm not pregnant," she said flatly. "But I'll text you once I know for sure."

She jerked her arm away from me, and then turned and headed back toward the car.

I was hurt and angry, but I had to face the truth, deal with it.

She just didn't want…me.

There was no other goddamn reason that she didn't want to work this out somehow, and the last thing I wanted was to make a fool of myself over a woman who had wanted nothing except to experience the same pleasure we'd found together twelve years ago.

I wanted to deny it, but the only real excuse she had for brushing me off was because she didn't want a permanent place in my life. Maybe that's why she said she wasn't normal. She didn't want commitments or heavy responsibilities.

After taking a deep breath and then releasing it slowly, I followed her to my vehicle, determined to somehow salvage a tiny bit of pride.

Chapter 21

Harper

I spent my last day in Rocky Springs avoiding Blake. I'd told him I wasn't feeling well and wanted to take it easy.

But I knew he didn't buy my excuse.

God, it tore my heart apart to hurt him this way, but what choice did I really have? I couldn't make a permanent commitment to him, even though my heart had never wanted anything more. And I couldn't stand to be near him without begging him to take me, imperfections and all.

No, it was definitely better to stay away, but it hadn't been easy.

Once I realized he'd left the house to go check out things on the breeding ranch, I'd taken a swim in his indoor pool and then tried desperately to relax in the hot tub. I'd gone back upstairs and had taken a shower and then tried to read a book.

Nothing, and I mean nothing, could take my mind off the fact that I'd rather be hanging out at the ranch with Blake than doing anything else.

God, how had all this ever happened? How had I gotten to the point that leaving Blake felt like leaving a big part of my heart and soul behind me?

My heart was breaking as I finally tossed my book aside, everything inside me telling me that I should tell Blake the truth. Problem was, he would probably tell me it was okay that I wasn't normal, and that we could work it out.

But I knew there was no way to fix me, and I knew what would lie ahead for us as a couple would be an ugly road that could very well end up tearing us apart.

Blake deserved everything he wanted: love and a family of his own. He should have a wife who would make him her everything, and one capable of giving him all that he wanted.

I swiped at my tears angrily. Wishing I could be his was selfish. Yes, I wanted Blake. I had since the moment he'd come to rescue a silly eighteen-year-old girl from a homeless shelter all those years ago.

Problem was, things had changed since we'd met back then, and I no longer had a massive crush on him.

I was a woman, and I loved him with every fiber of my being. That more mature love made me ask myself if I wanted to give him part of the life he wanted, or if he should have it all.

The answer for me was simple. I loved him. Blake was worthy of having it all, and that didn't include a woman like me.

I was restless as hell, and I kept pacing my room, trying to figure out what to do with myself. I thought about going out hiking, but I'd noticed what looked like freezing rain coming down earlier and I was pretty certain it would probably turn to snow later if it kept falling.

Finally, I pulled on a pair of sweatpants, a T-shirt, and my sneakers, and then headed to the part of the house where I'd seen a gym.

If I didn't find a way to burn off some of my nervous energy, I swore I was going to lose it.

I'd only opened the door halfway when I heard a steady slapping noise coming fast and furious from inside the gym.

Blake? I'd thought he was still outside.

I nudged the door open a little more, and then peeked inside.

The gym was enormous for a home facility, with high ceilings, exercise mats, and plenty of pieces of equipment I'd never seen before. Not that I was exactly an exercise aficionado. My preference was to walk outside and see whatever sights I could see while getting my exercise, and I liked a good hike when I could get one.

I gaped as I watched the large man with his back to me jumping rope at a speed that made him and the rope both look like a blur. As I focused, the rope was still fuzzy because it was moving so fast, but I had no doubt who the powerful man was pounding away at jumping, his torso bare from the waist up, and only a pair of light sweatpants on his lower body.

Holding my breath, I wondered how long he'd keep up the punishing pace, but I finally had to release the air before I passed out. He went on and on, never slowing down for a moment.

Moving inside, I took a seat in the corner, hoping he wouldn't see me and I wouldn't interrupt his workout.

It seemed like it took forever for him to finally drop the rope, and I was surprised when he moved to a large punching bag suspended from the ceiling. He stood completely still for a moment before he began a series of kicks, his feet flying high as he hit several of the marks on the large bag. It would swing and then move back toward him, but he timed his kicks so well that it had barely come back toward him before he slammed it again. And again.

I watched him move with the grace of a ballerina and the force of an angry tiger. I cringed in the corner as he did an amazingly fluid and lightning-fast roundhouse kick, but I was pretty certain he had turned so fast that he didn't notice me.

Turns out, I was wrong.

He stopped and turned around, his hands on his hips and breathing heavily. "I thought you decided to hide in your room until you were ready to go," he said in a panting, husky tone.

I got to my feet, thinking about his question, but my eyes never left his toned body coated with a thin sheen of perspiration. "You did once tell me that you were into the martial arts. It looks like you still are."

I moved forward, realizing I really was doing the one thing I swore I'd never do again.

I was hiding, running away.

He grabbed a towel from a bench and scrubbed it over his face and down his upper body. "Taekwondo. Black belt. Yeah. I still try to keep up my skills. It's easier if I have a sparring partner, but Marcus is my only decent opponent, and he's obviously unavailable."

"So does that make you a lethal weapon"? I asked jokingly.

He tossed the towel in a basket next to the mat. "Never," he answered seriously. "If you meet somebody who truly practices the art, he or she would be the first one to walk away from a fight instead of escalating it. I use what I know only if I have to."

Blake was strong, powerful, yet he'd never use his strength and training to hurt someone if he could avoid it. I think I admired his attitude even more than his skills.

I shrugged. "I'm sorry I can't help you. I don't know the first thing about martial arts."

His gray eyes met mine and he nodded. "I know. You like to walk."

"I do, but it's sleeting, so I came down to see if I could find something else to do."

"Nervous energy?" he asked.

I nodded.

"Running away from things will do that sometimes," he answered solemnly.

"Blake, I—"

"Don't," he warned, his jaw clenched tightly. "Don't tell me that's not what you're doing."

"I won't," I answered grimly. "Because I'd be lying. I like to think I stopped running away, but I haven't. Not this time."

"Then why are you doing it?" He glared at me, the intensity of his stare compelling.

I squirmed uncomfortably. "Circumstances that are out of my control. I'm sorry."

"For fuck's sake, just tell me what's wrong, Harper. I'll do anything in my power to fix it. But please don't leave me again. Not this time."

I stared into his dark, tempestuous eyes, indecision making me freeze.

Could I actually tell him?

I'd already been over this in my mind a thousand times, but there was nothing good that could come from telling him why I had to go, why I couldn't continue our relationship.

"I have to go," I said as I lowered my eyes so I couldn't see his face.

He moved forward with lightning speed, tipping my chin up roughly so I was forced to look at him again. "Goddammit, this isn't you, Harper. You don't run, and you don't hide. We've been straight with each other from the beginning. You know damn well that I don't want to see this end between us. Not now. Not ever. What the hell else do you want me to say?"

My heart was pounding and my breath came in short spurts as I looked up at him, afraid my heart was in my eyes as I memorized his striking features and the fierce need in his eyes.

God, I hated myself so much for making him be the one to make himself vulnerable. It wasn't fair, because I needed him just as much as he needed me. But I loved him too much to keep him attached to me.

I shook my head slowly. "Nothing. I don't want you to say anything else."

"Fine," he said sharply. "Then I'll just take this."

His rapid motions had me down on the mat with him in moments, both of us kneeling and facing each other.

I wasn't sure how he'd even done it, but he hadn't hurt me at all.

Quickly snaking a hand behind my neck, he tugged me closer and lowered his head to kiss me.

Chapter 22

Harper

I was lost the moment our mouths fused and Blake started to plunder my lips, delving into my mouth with his tongue, completely owning me body and soul as I moaned into his mouth and wrapped my arms around his neck.

His skin was still moist and hot, and I stroked my hands across his back, savoring every moment of touching his bare skin.

He felt so warm and so alive. I whimpered quietly as he nipped my bottom lip, as though he was claiming me with every nibble to my skin and every lash of his tongue.

"Blake," I said longingly, tipping my head so he could put his mouth on every exposed inch of bare skin he could find.

He stood up suddenly. "If you're going to leave me, then by God I'll give you something to remember," he vowed as he kicked off his shoes and lowered the loose pants down to his ankles.

In moments, I was staring up at him, completely naked, my body shaking with need. Gut-wrenching desire swept over me and I grasped the hard cock that was right in front of my face. "We have unfinished business," I reminded him.

"Harper. Don't," he rasped.

I licked over the sensitive head while I held him firmly with my right hand. He wasn't shaking me off, so I knew he actually wanted me to continue.

His hands threaded through my hair, dislodging the clip and letting the locks cascade over my shoulders.

I went into a cadence that seemed to make him crazy as his hands tightened in my hair. He guided my movements as I tried to swallow him with every pump of his hips. I touched his balls with my free hand, teasing them before I reached back and caressed the tightest ass I could ever imagine.

He was groaning out my name, and that spurred me on. I swiped my free fingers through my own pussy and then stroked his ass again, this time using one of my damp fingers to push inside his puckered anus.

I didn't get far before resistance started, and I curled my finger a little to stroke inside him.

"Goddammit, Harper, I'm going to come." His voice was feral and unrecognizable.

He grasped my hair harder, and I kept moving my finger shallowly in and out of his ass while I tried to give him a blowjob he'd never forget.

His cock seemed to swell in my mouth, and he fisted my hair until it hurt. But finally, his seed flowed into my mouth, and I swallowed it, savoring the wild, erotic groans that exploded from him as he found an explosive release.

I licked his shaft clean and then smiled as he lowered himself to the mat and collapsed onto his back. "Christ! I think you killed me," he uttered as he tried to catch his breath.

I sat on the mat, watching him as his breathing slowed.

A few minutes later, he moved quickly and pinned my body under his before I could even think about moving away. "Why in the hell did you do that?" he rasped. "Why?"

I looked up at him and answered, "I just wanted to make you feel good."

"It did. But for the life of me, I don't fucking understand you," he rumbled before his mouth came crashing down on mine. "Women don't give head like that to a guy she never wants to see again."

What Blake didn't understand was that it wasn't that I didn't *want* to see him again. I *couldn't*.

He kissed me breathless, and my arms went around his damp shoulders, trying to give him everything in my heart and soul with that single embrace.

Rearing up, he pulled me into a sitting position and yanked the T-shirt over my head, and then stopped before he tossed it away. "This is my T-shirt," he said incredulously. "The one I let you use twelve years ago."

"I kept it," I admitted.

No matter how many years had passed, for some reason I'd never been able to throw away that old T-shirt. Maybe because it was the only thing I had that belonged to him.

Blake tossed it off the mat, and then removed the rest of my loose clothing and threw it in the pile.

I gasped as he came back to me and lowered his body down until we met skin-to-skin.

"You can run, Harper, but know that I'm always going to find you," he promised in a graveled tone, lifting my legs and wrapping them around his waist. "We were fucking meant to be like this."

With one thrust, he smoothly glided into my sheath, stretching me with his girth until I was full of him, full of Blake.

"Yesssss!" I hissed erotically, my reaction completely carnal and primitive. "Fuck me. Please."

I didn't argue that we weren't meant to be joined together. The sensation was so profound that there was no use denying the truth.

We were meant to be together.

We were once fated.

But reality was going to tear us apart.

"Feel me, Harper. Tell me this doesn't feel right," he growled.

"Fuck me," I answered. "I know how right it feels."

For now, he had won. I was lost to every single touch, beguiled by every thrust of his massive cock as he claimed me more thoroughly than I ever could have thought possible.

Our bodies rocked together frantically, both of us rising higher and higher, closer and closer to our ultimate pleasure.

Part of me wanted to slow down and enjoy the moment, but Blake was driving the punishing pace, grinding against my wet pussy with every brutal stroke.

My orgasm hit me hard and fast, leaving me helplessly shuddering to completion as I screamed his name, "Blake. Yes. Harder."

"You're so damn hot for me, baby," he groaned. "Let yourself come."

I did, and I clung to him as spasm after spasm gripped my body in a nearly painful climax. I didn't close my eyes because I wanted to watch him. As he reared up and grasped my thighs and then threw his head back as he pounded into me a few more times, I noticed the agonized look on his face before it left my sight. His neck muscles strained as he leaned his head back and found his own powerful release.

He collapsed on top of me, and I welcomed his weight as he panted harshly above me.

"I'm not letting you go, Harper. I won't. I can't."

I pushed hard on his chest. "Not tonight, okay?" I pleaded. "Come with me. Shower and sleep with me."

It was my last night, and all I really wanted was to be close to him. It didn't matter that the memories would torture me later. I wanted to live for tonight because it was all I had.

He got up and held his hand out, and I took it, letting him pull me to my feet.

"We did it again. No fucking condom," he mentioned coarsely.

"Don't think about it right now," I requested in a pleading voice and put my fingers over his lips. "If something happens, I'll let you know."

He nodded, and then picked me up and cradled my naked body in his arms as he stalked out of the gym and to his bedroom.

Very few words were spoken that night. Everything was said with our bodies, and I slept, completely exhausted, in his arms until the next morning.

Chapter 23

Harper

"Please don't tell me that you snuck out without telling Blake good-bye," Dani said in a disappointed voice as she sprawled out on the couch of my temporary lodgings in Boston. She was looking at a magazine article, but I knew damn well she was listening to everything I was saying.

I flopped into a chair of the furnished condo with a bag of potato chips, shoveling them into my mouth without even thinking about what I was eating.

Dani had arrived yesterday, and seeing her face had been about the only thing that could make me happy right now. "I didn't *sneak out,*" I objected, even though I so *had* snuck out. I wasn't sure I could handle saying good-bye to Blake. I was also terrified that if I did, I'd break down and tell him everything. "I had an early morning flight, and I needed to return my rental. I needed to leave early and I didn't want to wake him."

Dani looked up from her magazine and tossed it aside, rolling her eyes as she looked at me. "You're so full of shit. You wimped out. Why?"

For having been a captive in deplorable conditions, Dani looked good. Her face was still bruised and she was incredibly thin. But she was eating like a horse, and I was pretty certain she'd gain her weight back quickly. She'd gotten her hair cut into a very cute pixie, a style that made her eyes look enormous and gorgeous.

I'd had to get on her case several times about resting. She wanted to go out and explore Boston, which probably meant she wanted to find a good story, but she needed to rest for a while. Her broken ribs were still hurting her pretty badly, even though she rarely complained.

"Why?" Dani asked again when I didn't answer.

"Okay. Yeah." I stuffed more chips in my mouth before I answered. "I was afraid."

"You're in love with him, right?"

I nodded slowly as I continued to munch on my chips.

"Harper, I understand why you're hesitant, but when I thought I was going to die, the unimportant things didn't matter anymore. The only thing that I really cared about was the people I loved, and how much I wanted to get back to them. I had regrets, maybe because there were so many things that I didn't try hard enough to resolve." She stood and stretched, snatching the bag of chips from me before dropping back slowly onto the couch.

"Dani, you know why I can't marry him," I argued.

She chewed a mouthful of food before responding. "Honestly, Harper, no, I don't. If you cut through all the bullshit and put the truth out there, he either loves you enough or he doesn't. It's pretty simple. It sounds like you never even gave him a chance. That's so unfair, and you're the fairest and kindest person I know."

"If I did, I know he'd say it was okay, and we'd deal with it," I said sadly. "But I don't think it would be okay. He'd end up regretting his choice when the newness wears off."

"Oh, for God's sake, you don't know that. When in the hell did you become such a pessimist? That's my job."

I was usually upbeat and positive, but I didn't feel that way right now. I felt brokenhearted, depressed, and so lonely that my soul was crying out for Blake. "Since I fell in love with a man who deserves the world," I answered solemnly.

"He deserves *you*. It sounds like you *are* his world." Dani retorted. "Happiness is never guaranteed, Harper. Hell, how do you know he won't die tomorrow? How do you know you won't? Any of us could be gone from this Earth in an instant. I swore I'd never let myself be held back from anything I wanted ever again. I don't want to have regrets," she told me. "And I don't want you to have any either."

I already had regrets, and every one of them involved Blake Colter. "What if he ends up resenting me?" I asked her.

"What if he doesn't? What if he never gets married because he couldn't have the woman he wanted? You told me you've been the only woman he's wanted for twelve years. The guy was basically in his prime, and he didn't want to run around spreading his seed everywhere. What if he still feels that way?"

I frowned. "I guess I never considered the fact that Blake wouldn't ever find a woman to love. He'd be most women's dream guy."

"He loves *you*," Dani replied with a mouthful of chips. "If he hasn't even dated another woman, why would he now?"

Now that I'd had a few days to think, I realized that I should have told Blake the whole truth and let the chips fall on the table, wherever they were meant to land. Now that I was away from the emotional torment of being close to him, I knew I was never going to get over Blake Colter. I loved him just that much.

He'd said he'd been waiting for me. Deep inside, I knew I'd been waiting, too. Time had passed and life had gone on, but there was always something missing, a gaping hole inside me that was empty without him. "Maybe I should have handled it differently," I confessed.

"Like, maybe you should have told him why you're really scared?"

I watched as Dani got up and went to the fridge to find more food. "I'll make you something healthy," I told her as I rushed to the kitchen.

"Really, sis?" she said jokingly. "After being a captive and nearly starved, the last thing I want is something healthy. How about pizza?"

"We'd have to order out," I said absently.

"Works for me," Dani agreed and snagged a soda from the fridge.

I called the pizza place that we'd seen down the street, and ordered half the menu. It looked like my depressive eating was going to keep going on for a while, and Dani *did* need to gain weight.

Dani snorted as I hung up the phone. "Not that I'm complaining, but do we *really* need that much food? I mean, you could have backed off on the desserts. I think we'll be pretty full with several pizzas, hot wings, sandwiches, and whatever else you ordered."

"You need to put on weight," I told her defensively.

"I'll gain it back soon enough. If I stay here for another week, I think I'll gain it all back," she teased.

I wanted to glare at her, but ended up smiling as I saw her mischievous grin. Dani had been upbeat and happy since she'd gotten to Boston. She'd shared some of the terror she'd experienced during the kidnapping, and she said they hadn't sexually abused her. But some of the psychological torment they'd put her through had been pretty horrifying.

"Are you going back to your network?" I asked carefully. I didn't want to encourage her. Personally, I wished she had a different career, a safer one.

"When I'm ready," she answered. "The bosses won't even hear about it until I've taken a very long vacation. They don't want to be accused of dragging a hero back to work until she's completely healed," she relayed in a disgusted tone.

"Are you going to be okay with going back to the same position?"

She nodded. "I will. But I'll never take anything for granted again."

"You were always cautious," I said, feeling like I wanted to support her.

"I was. Unfortunately, Marcus the Prick says I'm reckless. He threatened to be around every time I have a new assignment. What is he planning on doing? Being my nanny?"

I laughed. "Marcus is anything but somebody's nanny. He's pretty cold."

"Not always," Dani remarked. "He has his good moments. Granted, there aren't many of them between the times that he's a jackass, but there is some kindness deep down."

"I'm sure there is," I agreed. "He rescued you, and he didn't have to. Even Tate risked his own butt."

"Tate's a good man," Dani said appreciatively. "Marcus is way too uptight. Is Blake anything like him?"

I shook my head. "They look identical, but their personalities are different. Blake isn't afraid to be kind, and he likes people. Maybe that's what makes him a good senator. He's sweet, and he's passionate about what he thinks is right and wrong. He has a scientific mind, and he's brilliant. He's also patient. He would make a wonderful father someday."

Dani went back to flop on the couch, and I returned to my recliner as she mused, "If he's patient, then he and Marcus are very different."

"He also has a pretty good sense of humor. And a smile that could charm a woman out of her panties," I admitted.

"But he only uses it on you," Dani joked. "Harper, how long is it going to take you to go see the guy and throw yourself on his mercy for sneaking out on him?"

"I did not sneak," I said in a haughty voice. "I just…left."

"Harper," Dani said in a chastising voice.

I looked at her disappointed expression and said, "I know you're right. Now that I've had some space, I realize what I did wasn't fair. I was scared that he'd reject me. I was afraid that I couldn't give him what he wanted. I was afraid that my issues would eventually ruin our relationship, and make him unhappy."

"You need to at least give him a chance. If you don't, you'll never know how he'll feel. I saw him in passing when I was leaving Washington. I'm telling you, the poor guy looked haunted and miserable. He certainly wasn't smiling."

My head jerked up and looked at her. "You saw Blake?"

"Yeah. I was boarding Marcus's plane as he was leaving his private jet. We passed right by each other, but he didn't even know who I was. I think he was lost in his own world."

I frowned. "I don't know what to do," I whispered aloud, the pain in my voice unhidden.

"Go. See. Him," Dani insisted. "DC is a short hop, and we have three brothers who all have a private jet, or you could hire your own. You could be there in a little over an hour."

I wasn't going anywhere until Dani was on the mend. "I'll think about it," I promised.

"Think hard," she suggested. "I hate seeing you like this, and everything that happened in the past is out of your control. You deserve to be happy just as much as Blake does. You just don't see that."

The doorbell rang, and I motioned her to stay put. She'd been up and down enough for one day.

I looked through the peephole and saw the poor pizza guy struggling to juggle all the food I had ordered.

I went for my wallet, knowing the poor guy deserved a very big tip.

Chapter 24

Blake

For the first time since I'd become a senator, I knew I'd been distracted during the session earlier in the day.

I hated myself for that.

I had a job to do, but I couldn't seem to get my head on straight. Since the moment I'd woken up and found out that Harper had left to go to Boston, I hadn't been myself.

I went from being depressed to periods of anger, not sure if I wanted to yell at Harper or beg her to come back.

My pride didn't matter anymore. Some things were worth more than avoiding humiliation.

"I got it," Marcus said as he came into my historic home in Georgetown, my residence when I was working in Washington.

I could probably have been closer to Capitol Hill, but I preferred the charm of a historic residence over a contemporary condo. It felt more like home when I was staying here.

I turned from the process of making myself a drink to look at him. "Got what?"

Going back to filling my tumbler, I made one for Marcus, too.

"I got Harper's current address in Boston. You know you're going there as soon as this session is over," Marcus answered, sounding like he was daring me to deny that I was going to run after her again.

I nodded. "Good. I'm glad you found her address. It will save me some time." *Fuck my pride.* I didn't care anymore if I made an ass out of myself. Somehow, I was getting Harper back. Whatever problems she had with commitment, I'd resolve them. The last thing I wanted was to hold her back. All I wanted was to love her, and have her fucking love me back.

Marcus smirked and dropped the piece of paper on a small side table. "Couldn't you have just asked her? You have her cell, right?"

I did have her current number, but I hadn't been able to bring myself to call her. If she was going to ditch me completely, I was going to make her do it in person. "Phone calls have never worked well for us in the past," I replied as I held out a tumbler of good Scotch to Marcus. "And I doubt she'd tell me her address if she answered."

"Are you sure you want to chase this woman?" Marcus asked doubtfully.

"Yes," I answered brusquely.

"Why in the hell did she ditch you anyway?"

"I wish I knew," I answered with a heavy sigh. "But something isn't right, and I need to find out what's going on. Harper isn't the type to just run away. If she didn't want me, she'd have no problem telling me to my face. Something is holding her back. Something is bothering her. I just don't know what the hell the problem is."

"Do you want me to do some digging?" Marcus suggested.

"Yes…No…" Did I want to know? Hell, yeah. But I wanted to hear it from Harper. "No. I need her to tell me herself. No more misunderstandings."

"Okay. But call me if you need anything else," Marcus said gruffly. "I'm headed back to Rocky Springs."

"I'll be back to Colorado soon. Things will either go well in Boston or they won't." I'd been in DC for almost two weeks, and we'd have a break before we convened again.

"Good luck," Marcus said grimly as he drained his glass and then headed toward the door.

"I'll need it." I followed him out to his car and driver and then watched as the limo cruised down the street and disappeared.

Tomorrow morning, I'd be headed for Boston, and I was determined to drag information out of Harper—mainly why the hell she'd left, and why she was so damn unwilling to even try to make our relationship work.

Every damn day I wanted her more, and the need was eating me up inside. Harper had always been the part of me that was missing. It had just taken seeing her again to realize it.

Finishing my drink, I sat the glass in the sink at the bar, then turned to make my way upstairs. I needed to pack some stuff and then get headed out early in the morning.

I raced up the steps, hoping to hell that I could finally break down Harper's defenses and make her spill out the information I needed.

Harper

Dani hung out with me for a week before she left to go visit our brothers. Once she was gone, all I had was my own company, and I hated it.

It didn't take me long to decide that I needed to stop running away from Blake. I had to tell him, and deal with whatever emotional fallout came from that decision.

My sister was right. Life was way too short for this kind of bullshit.

I was avoiding.

I was running from something good.

Yeah, I could end up rejected or even resented eventually, but at least there would be no more confusion for Blake about how I felt.

I loved him. He'd been the only guy for me since the first time I'd been with him. He obviously felt the same way since he'd actually shunned every woman who looked his way or tried to get his attention for the last twelve years.

I'd lamented for several days about exactly what to do, and I'd finally decided I needed to see him in person.

I was going to Washington. My brother, Jett, had scoped out Blake's address in Georgetown, and he'd sent his own jet for me to use for transport.

At the end of the day, Blake was either going to be mine, or I'd be heartbroken. But it was far better than not knowing what would have happened if I'd just told him.

Dani had been right when she'd said that I deserved to be happy, and what happened years ago had been out of my control. I didn't need to feel broken, and I never had until I'd become so damn vulnerable. I'd come to terms with how my life would be…but then I'd seen Blake again, and everything I felt had turned me upside down all over again.

But I was ready now. My sister was safe, so I wasn't whirling around in a constant state of fear. I'd finally gotten my head together enough to know what I wanted, and what I had to do to get it.

I had to take a huge risk with my heart, but Blake was worth it.

I fidgeted as I waited for Jett's plane to take off. It was the height of luxury, with cream leather seats and a bedroom in the back, but I hardly noticed. All I wanted to do was get to Blake right now and spill the secrets I'd been keeping.

I sighed as the jet went airborne.

What if he doesn't want to talk to me?

What if he doesn't want me after he knows?

Why is it that negative thoughts have to intrude just when a person decides they're going to lay their heart on the line?

So much of this decision was made by listening to Dani talk over the last week, discussing her encounters with her captors, and how she never wanted any regrets. I realized how little I was actually enjoying my life. I was fulfilled by the things I did, but my heart and soul was otherwise empty, and I didn't want to continue that way.

Not if I didn't have to be alone.

Not if Blake cared enough.

I refused any food or drink from the flight attendant, my stomach in knots. Jett had a car waiting for me at the airport, and I tried to take deep, calming breaths on my way to Blake's house.

When we arrived, I took my carry-on suitcase and thanked the driver with a massive tip, and then made my way to the door. I might be terrified, but I couldn't help but notice the row of historic homes, each one more impressively preserved than the rest.

I loved that Blake had chosen a home over living in a condo closer to the Hill. The architect in me wanted to take a walk and check out the preservations that had been made to all of the houses, but I had more pressing issues to deal with at the moment.

I rang the doorbell and then waited until somebody finally opened the door.

Unfortunately, it wasn't the face I'd been hoping to see.

The woman was middle-aged, and was holding a handheld sweeper.

"I'm looking for Blake Colter," I said hesitantly.

"He's not here, ma'am." The woman was polite but to the point.

Dammit! "He went back to Colorado?"

My cell phone started to ring, and I juggled my things to get it out. I answered in a breathless voice that was formed from fear and the disappointment that I'd missed him.

"Hello."

"Where in the hell are you?" Blake asked demandingly.

"Georgetown," I answered honestly. "I came to see you."

"Shit!" he cursed harshly. "I'm in Boston. I had to see you."

It took me a moment to realize that we were still in separate cities, although we'd both had the same idea of being in the same place.

I started to laugh, the lady who was apparently Blake's housekeeper staring at me like I was touched in the head.

On the other end of the line, I could tell that he was laughing, too.

"Unbelievable. We try to get to each other, and we end up in separate places," Blake said with humor in his tone.

I chuckled. "If you would have just stayed here..."

"Or if you would have just stayed in Boston. Don't go anywhere. I'll be there in a couple of hours," he demanded. "Is my housekeeper there?"

"Yes." I handed my cell phone to the bewildered woman still at the door.

She spoke to Blake for several minutes, mostly giving one- and two-word answers. When she finally hung up and handed my phone back to me, she stepped back. "Please come in. Senator Colter would like you to make yourself at home."

I entered, admiring the décor as I analyzed how well the architecture had been preserved. It was a lovely home. Not pretentious, but definitely designed with antiques to match the construction period.

She showed me into a family room that had newer furnishings, a space that was probably the most often used in the home. "Thank you," I murmured.

"Can I get you some food? Something to drink?"

Although I really wanted to keep up my compulsive eating and ask for food, I ended up answering, "No. I'm fine, thanks."

The woman retreated and closed the door behind her. I took off my jacket and the boots I was wearing and sat on the comfortable leather couch, still stunned that Blake had gone after me in Boston.

That gave me hope.

That made my heart lighter.

I flipped on the television and then covered myself with a throw blanket.

I tried to stay awake and focused, but I'd barely slept for the last few nights, and I was exhausted.

A few minutes later, I couldn't keep my eyes open, and I slept.

Chapter 25

Blake

My flight back to the DC area seemed like the longest period of time I'd ever known. Even though the hop was short, I was restless throughout the whole flight, hoping to hell Harper would still be at my house when I got there.

As I finally climbed the stairs of my historic mansion, I took a deep breath as I put the key into the lock, my heart hammering with anticipation.

What if she doesn't want me?

What if this is the last time I see her?

I pushed the negative thoughts from my head as I entered the home and everything was deathly quiet. My housekeeper was obviously gone, and as I strolled through the formal living room, I could hear the television from the family room.

This was it. Time to fight for what I really wanted, really needed. My life wasn't worth a shit without Harper, and I needed to make her understand that no matter what was standing in our way, I'd make it go away.

Pushing the door open, I peered inside, looking from the television mounted on the wall to the leather couch where Harper was laying, looking so comfortable that even before I approached, I knew she was asleep.

Jesus, she looked beautiful. Her hair was down and partially covering her face. Without thought, I crouched down and pushed back the strands, revealing her delicate features as she slept.

The dark smudges under her eyes told me she'd probably slept as much as I had for at least the last few days, but otherwise, she looked gorgeous.

Mine!

It seemed so perfectly natural for her to be here that my heart clenched as I saw her shoes, purse, and jacket on the chair.

"She has to stay," I said to myself huskily as I pulled the blanket around her body.

I stroked her hair lightly, and she stirred. "Blake," she said in a sleep-laden, groggy voice.

"Sleep, Harper. We can talk later. I'm here."

I heard her sigh, and then her breathing fell into an even cadence again. Her trust in me had my heartbeat kicking up as I stared down at her.

I moved to a chair beside the sofa, kicked off my shoes, and just watched her sleep.

Harper

I could sense Blake's presence the moment I started to wake. My eyes fluttered open, and I almost immediately met his steely-eyed stare.

"You're here." *Brilliant, right?* It was pretty damn obvious that he was home. I was staring right at him.

"I've been here awhile. I wanted to let you get some rest."

I struggled to sit up, wiping the sleep from my eyes. "When did you get in?"

He shrugged. "A few hours ago."

"You should have woken me. I'm sorry. I was so tired, I fell asleep."

"I know the feeling," he answered coarsely. "I haven't slept much, either."

As I stared at him, still trying to get my bearings, it was obvious that he was tired. His dark hair was almost standing on end in several places, like he'd been running his hand through his hair in frustration. His usually-sharp gaze was dulled, and his jaw was scruffy, like he hadn't shaved in a day or two.

Even in his state of disarray, the custom suit with the missing tie and the top few buttons of his shirt open, Blake was still the most beautiful sight I'd seen in a long time. My heart stuck in my throat as I looked at the genuine sadness in his eyes, and all I wanted to do was fix whatever was wrong.

I wanted everything to be right in his world again, especially since I knew that I'd been the one to cause him to be in this state. I recognized his sorrow. It cried out to me because it echoed my own.

"I'm so sorry," I said, hoping the emotion in those three little words would help to undo the hurt I'd caused him.

And I *had* hurt him. The torment was written all over his face.

"Why did you leave me, Harper? Why?" His voice was both angry and pleading, demanding to know why I'd run away.

"Because I can't be everything for you, Blake. I can't be the woman you need," I began to explain.

"You're fucking everything to me," he interrupted forcefully. "Everything."

"But I'm not long-term relationship material," I argued. "I'm not a woman you can live happily-ever-after with."

"Why the hell not? Jesus, Harper, I've waited for twelve damn years just to see you again. Maybe I never consciously admitted that to myself until I saw you again, but it's true." He got up and came to sit on the couch, and then grabbed me by the shoulders so I'd look at him. "You think I haven't had my chances to settle for somebody else? Fuck other women? Get laid just to get off?"

I looked at his frenzied expression. "I know you have, and I know you could."

"But I damn well didn't," he rasped. "You want to know why?"

I couldn't speak, so I nodded.

"Because I could never, ever fall out of love with you. It didn't matter how much I tried—you've haunted me for over a fucking decade. One night with you, and I was ruined. You yanked my heart out of my chest and kept it all of this time. I never once wanted anybody else. It's always been you."

Tears trickled down my cheeks as I answered, "I felt the same way."

"Then tell me why in the hell you can't stay. I love you, Harper. I always have."

I felt the knife slash into my chest, a pain so intense that I had to put my hand to my heart to make sure it really hadn't been shattered. "This is all wrong, Blake. So wrong."

He shook me lightly. "What? Just tell me what in the hell is so damn wrong. I'll fix it. I'll make it right."

I swiped at my tears angrily as I replied, "You can't make it right. Nobody can."

"Tell me."

"You'd make an amazing father," I told him in a voice filled with pain.

"Yeah. And I'd love to get you pregnant if that's what you want. In case you haven't noticed, practicing is no problem for me."

"That's the issue. You can't and you never will." I took a deep breath and met his stare head-on. "I can't have children, Blake. Never. And you can't fix that."

There was complete silence in the room as Blake just sat and stared at me, looking puzzled. "Why?"

"I got pregnant twelve years ago. I know you used a condom, but something went wrong."

"Do we have a child?" Blake asked cautiously.

I shook my head slowly. "No."

"Old condoms," he replied. "One of my buddies at college gave them to me once he'd found a girlfriend and was having a committed relationship. His girlfriend was on birth control. I don't know how long he'd had them, but when I saw the box after I went back to college, they were expired. Latex breaks down after a certain amount of time has passed. I didn't think much more about it because I never heard from you again." He hesitated before he questioned in a gruff tone, "Why didn't you call me? What happened?"

I took a deep breath and let it out, trying to relax before I explained. "I lost the baby. I had what's called an ectopic pregnancy, where the fertilized egg gets stuck in the fallopian tube. It ruptured and I had to have emergency surgery. I can't have children anymore, Blake. I'm infertile."

I saw the flash of his eyes, and I could almost hear the questions forming in his mind. I'd wanted to make the explanation simple, but I could tell I wasn't going to get away without answering more questions.

Chapter 26

Harper

"Did you know you were pregnant?" Blake's eyes were fierce and his jaw was set tight as he asked the question.

"I'd just found out," I explained. "I'd barely come to terms with the fact that I was pregnant. And yes, I was going to tell you. You had the right to know. But I never got that far before I had to have surgery. The pregnancy was never viable. I found out after I had surgery that I had endometriosis in both of my tubes, and they were blocked. The doctor removed one of them, and tried to clean the other, but I have scar tissue now, and my gynecologist tested to see if an egg would pass. He said the chances are almost nil."

"There are other ways. IVF?"

"Possible, but difficult. Blake, after I lost the baby, I was depressed. Despondent. I'm not sure I can go through something like that again. I wasn't myself for several years."

He took off his suit jacket and tossed it on the chair, and then put his arms around me and pulled me into his lap. "Did you want the baby when you thought the pregnancy was normal?"

I looked at him with puffy, red eyes, my tears still flowing. "Yes. Once I got used to the idea I was pregnant, I wanted it very much. I had the means to support the baby and still go to school, and I wanted it because..." I wasn't even sure how to explain.

"Because it was ours," he finished.

I nodded. "Because it was yours," I corrected. "I couldn't quite admit that to myself back then, but I know that it's true."

He used his thumb to wipe away some of the droplets from my cheeks as he asked, "Did you think for even a moment that you not being able to have a child would make any difference in the way I feel about you?"

"It makes a difference to me," I admitted. "You said you wanted to be a father, and you'd make an amazing dad."

"I don't give a damn, Harper. I hate that you suffered, and I wish to hell you would have called me so I could have been there for you. But under the circumstances, I get why you didn't. But we aren't college kids anymore, and all I ever really wanted was you."

"You're going to want a family, Blake," I protested.

"I can't have one without you," he said huskily, his eyes pleading with me to understand.

"You can't have one *with* me either," I said uncertainly.

"Harper, you're everything to me. If I don't have you, then I'll have nothing."

"I love you," I blurted out, unable to contain my emotions any longer. *God, I loved this strong, stubborn man who wouldn't, and never had, let go.*

I felt his big body shudder against mine. "I love you, too, baby. I've been trying to make you understand that since the moment I saw you again. There is no other woman for me. Never has been, and never will be."

I wrapped my arms around his neck and hugged him tightly, resting my head on his shoulder. "So we're basically screwed?"

"Sweetheart, I've been screwed since the day you looked up at me at that homeless shelter. But if you say you'll be mine, I'll be very happily screwed."

I smacked his arm. "This isn't something you can decide lightly, Blake. If you have me, you'll probably not have any children."

"Why can't we just adopt a child, one of those homeless kids who need parents? Harper, a child doesn't need my DNA for me to love him or her, and for us to be parents." He nuzzled my neck, trying to comfort me.

I'd always wanted to adopt a child, and I'd planned on doing it as a single parent once I settled down. For many of the children who needed a home, one stable parent was much better than none. But the fact that Blake really didn't seem to care if the child was a natural child of his made my heart soar with a happiness I hadn't even dared believe could exist.

I could have Blake.

And we could have our family.

All I had to do was believe he'd be content with that.

I leaned back and tilted my head, staring into his warm, gray eyes, my heart melting like butter. "You could live with us never having a child of our own?"

"What's the point of going through the process of trying to have one of our own when so many kids need a home?" he asked, sounding genuinely perplexed.

"God, you're such an amazing man, Blake Colter," I told him in an awed voice.

"I'm not that great," he discounted. "Plenty of people adopt."

Yeah. They did. But it was usually a decision that was made when there was no other option, or if they wanted to add to their family. But my wonderful, beautiful Blake wanted to do it just because it felt right. "I love you. I love you for your support, your understanding, and your generous heart. I love that you can accept me, even if I'm a little bit broken."

"You. Are. Not. Broken." His voice was graveled and raw. "Harper, I got you pregnant, and then I wasn't there for you. You were seriously ill, and who was there?"

"Nobody," I answered honestly. "I didn't want my parents to know, and it happened so fast. The only one who knows is Dani, and I didn't tell her until years later, when I knew I had too much scar tissue to be fertile."

He pulled me back against his body and held me there, stroking a hand over my hair. "Stay with me, Harper. Never leave me again. I want to be there when you need me. I want you to marry me, and we *will* live happily-ever-after. I promise you. All I really need is you. Anything more is a bonus."

"I love you," I rasped into his shoulder. "I love you so much. I wanted you to have everything."

"I do," he said hoarsely. "I have her right here in my arms, and this time, she isn't going anywhere."

"No, I'm not." I sighed happily. "Not at the moment, anyway. I do have to be back in Boston in a few days."

He lifted me and placed a leg on each side of him until I was straddling him. "Then I guess I'd better get busy."

I smiled down at him, a grin of pure happiness. "Doing what exactly?"

"Convincing you that if you marry me, I'll keep you so happy that you'll never feel like you're missing out on anything," he answered earnestly.

Oh, God. Like I'd be living anything except my wildest dream if Blake was mine? "And how do you plan on doing that, Senator Colter?" I asked mischievously.

"By making you come until you can't move, even if you wanted to," he informed me with a sexy grin.

My heart was racing as I started to unbutton his shirt slowly. "Maybe it should be my job to keep you happy. I am the one who left, and I desperately want to be with you for the rest of our lives," I suggested.

"Don't get me wrong, I'm all for you doing that, but baby, all you really have to do is breathe to keep me wanting you. I've never stopped." His voice was low and sinfully carnal.

When I reached the last button, I pulled his shirt open and put my palms on his muscular chest. Blake was hard all over, and all I wanted to do was melt into his warm, protective body. "I never stopped, either."

He stood and pulled me up with him, holding me until I had my feet on the floor. He let me go to shrug out of his shirt, and I made short work of stripping right in front of him, letting him know that I had no secrets left. I was his, ready to bare myself to him—quite literally as well as figuratively.

I vowed that there would never be secrets between us again. If Blake could handle the fact that I could never have a child so effortlessly, then there was nothing we couldn't handle together.

He watched me with a feral gaze as I got naked, removing the rest of his clothing without taking his stare away from me.

The air around us was sparking with sexual tension, but neither one of us spoke. We communicated with our bodies and our eyes. He understood exactly what I was trying to convey, and the moment I'd dropped my last article of clothing, he opened his arms.

I flowed into him, biting my lip to keep from moaning as we met skin-to-skin, and I wrapped my arms around his waist and stroked my hands up the heated skin of his back as he fisted a handful of my hair to jerk my head back so he could devour me with a kiss as carnal as he'd ever given me.

My body responded almost violently, turned on by how much he needed me and how vulnerable we were to each other.

I moaned into his mouth, desperate for him to join our bodies, but he released my lips and held onto my hair, trailing his mouth over every inch of bare skin he could find.

"Blake. Please. I need you," I whimpered, spearing my hands into his hair.

My emotions were overflowing my body, and I needed an outlet fast.

"You'll get me. Every inch," he rasped, stepping back so his hands could cup my breasts, teasing each nipple before he moved down and delved his fingers between my thighs.

"Yes," I breathed out encouragingly. "Touch me."

I was already slick and ready for him, and I felt his body tense as his fingers slid easily through my folds. "Baby, you're so ready for me."

"I've been ready." I slid my hand between us and palmed his hard cock.

"Don't, Harper," he groaned, pulling my hand away from him. "Right now I have to be inside you."

He grasped me around the waist, picked me up, and moved me over to a console table, placing my hands flat on the surface after he let my feet touch the floor. "Hold on," he demanded while he urged me to spread my legs with his feet.

I knew what he was going to do, and I was so ready for him, my core clenching at the thought of taking him as deeply inside me as possible.

I shivered in anticipation as he moved behind me, his hands stroking down my back and then my ass. His hand dipped between my parted thighs, massaging my clit sensually as I waited helplessly for him to take me.

"Blake. Please," I begged, needing this to go hot, hard, and fast to sate the ache inside me.

He grasped a handful of my hair again, pulling my head up. "Watch," he insisted. "Look at us while I make you come."

I hadn't noticed the mirror on the wall until he brought it to my attention. My eyes darted to his face. He was already watching me, and our eyes met and held in the mirror.

Blake's naked desire and his molten silver eyes devoured my wanton image, and I had nothing to hide. Not anymore. I loved this man fiercely, and I'd never hold back my emotions from him again.

I shot a covetous look back at him and demanded, "Fuck. Me. Now."

He snapped, his rough hands grabbing my hips, and with one quick thrust, he buried himself deep inside me, stretching me until I moaned with satisfaction. "Oh, God. Yes."

I kept my head up myself, avidly watching Blake's expression turn wild and hungry, the tension building as he pulled back and then surged into me again. "So wet. So tight. Jesus, Harper. I can't get enough."

"Take it all. Everything you want," I encouraged him in a breathless voice, needing Blake to finally, after all these years, claim me forever.

"Mine." The one word left his mouth covetously.

"Yes. I've always been yours. Take me."

He started pummeling into me almost savagely, but I welcomed the punishing force and pace.

I needed this.

I needed him.

The harder he thrust, the fiercer our need, and my hands slid forward to grasp the outside edges of the solid wood console, feeling like I was losing my mind as our harsh breath and the sound of our bodies meeting were the only sounds in the room.

I felt my climax building to a strength that almost scared me as Blake's face turned volatile and uncontrolled.

His hand slid from my hip to the front of my body, his fingers boldly delving into my pussy and stroking my clit as he continued his frenzied rhythm with his cock.

"Blake. Oh, God. I can't," I screamed.

"You can. Come for me," he commanded.

I looked into the mirror, not quite recognizing myself in the carnal image as my orgasm took control of my body, rocking it to its core.

"Blake! I love you! I love you!" The words left my mouth in a scream of ecstasy that I couldn't control.

"Yeah, sweetheart. Come for me."

The pulsations were so intense, the spasms so strong that I could barely stay on my feet as Blake pounded into me a few more times before he finally found his own release with a groan. "I love you, Harper. It's always been just you."

I shuddered at his words and in the final throes of my climax, Blake pulled me back against his body, wrapping his arms securely around my waist so I wouldn't fall.

He disconnected us and lifted me up, carrying me back to the couch before he put me back down again with my naked body draped over him.

I laid my head on his chest and listened as his heartbeat returned to a slower pace, my body sated and my heart filled with so much joy I could hardly breathe. I nuzzled his whiskered jawline and his neck. "Love you," I repeated, not able to tell him enough now that I'd finally said the words.

"I love you, too. And we're getting married," he said gruffly, wrapping his arms protectively around my body.

I smiled. With no reason to object anymore, I answered, "Yes. Yes, we are. I'm never running away again."

"Thank fuck," he said in a relieved voice.

I laughed, wondering what his constituents would say if they could hear him cursing so freely.

He yawned, and I knew he was really exhausted. "Don't you have a perfectly good bed here?"

He grinned up at me. "I do. A nice one. Would you like to see it?"

"Absolutely."

He rose with me in his arms and a happy grin on his face that made my heart stutter.

Blake showed me his bedroom, and he *did* have a perfectly good bed.

Knowing I'd be sharing it with Blake forever made it better than good; it was spectacular.

Epilogue

Harper

Two Months Later…

"I'm pregnant." There was no way to really ease into the fact that I was going to have Blake's child, so I just threw it out there.

I'd waited until we could be back together in Rocky Springs to break the news to him in person. The ultrasound had confirmed that the egg had passed through the scarred tube against the odds, and I now had his baby growing in my womb. I'd been terrified when I went to get the scan, so afraid that I'd end up with another tubal pregnancy, but the worst hadn't happened. After that, I'd been so excited to tell Blake that I'd almost blurted it out over the phone on my way back from Boston to Colorado.

We were both fine with adopting, but this happy event just seemed like icing on an already very sweet cake.

The last two months had been crazy, both of us bending over backward to meet up whenever we could. I missed him so damn much when we weren't together that my heart ached. So even if it was only for a day or two, I'd fly to Washington to see him, or he'd come to Boston just to spend a free day with me.

It had been the happiest period of time in my life. Blake spoiled me rotten, showering me with love and sweet little things that he'd picked up just because they somehow reminded him of me. I gave him back the love that he gave me, and did little things just to see him smile.

And he smiled often, making my heart skitter every single time. I had no doubt he was happy. And I'd be ecstatic if I never saw his beautiful eyes tortured and tormented ever again.

He turned and looked at me, forgetting all about the drink he was making to come back to the couch and sit beside me. "Did you really just say that you're pregnant?" he asked, confused.

"I guess I should have said we're pregnant," I corrected with a tremulous smile.

"Shit! We have to go to the hospital," he said in a worried voice as he started to rise.

I snagged his shirt, forcing him to sit back down. "You don't understand. I'm fine. I had an ultrasound. I'm pregnant. A normal pregnancy for now. The doctor says it happens. Sometimes the tube doesn't show as patent, but the egg makes it through."

I watched as he raked a worried hand through his hair, causing those few unruly strands I loved so much to stand straight up on his head.

"Are you safe?" he asked, his brow still furrowed with concern.

My heart tripped as I saw the fear in his expression. I took his hand in mine as I reassured him, "It's fine. I'm fine. But we're going to be parents a little sooner than we planned."

He looked pretty proud of himself as he finally started to grin. "We made a baby." He said the words like we were the only couple to accomplish such a feat.

He moved our conjoined hands to rest on my still-flat abdomen.

If I didn't have such a serious infertility issue, I probably would have laughed. Since we spent a whole lot of time in the act of mating, I would have inevitably ended up pregnant if I didn't have issues. "We certainly practice enough," I teased.

"I'm still worried," Blake confessed, his expression dumbfounded. "I want this baby, but I'm afraid something bad will happen to you."

My heart clenched, and my love for the man sitting beside me rushed up to smack me nearly speechless.

There was nothing wrong with me, and there was nothing wrong with the pregnancy. But Blake was still concerned about how it would affect me. "The hard and nearly impossible part is over. There's nothing wrong with my other female parts," I told him adamantly.

"Baby, I can attest to the fact that there was *never* anything wrong with your other female parts," he answered in a smart-ass tone.

I slapped him on the arm. "I'm serious, Blake. I'm going to be fine. Our baby will be fine. At this point, there's nothing wrong with either one of us."

He let out a masculine sigh of relief and pulled me onto his lap. "Nothing can ever happen to you, Harper. I'd never live through it." He hesitated before he asked, "Are you happy?"

I wrapped my arms around his neck, and he held me tightly, protectively. "Are you kidding? I'm ecstatic. We can still adopt later," I told him tenderly.

"We should never risk this happening again," he rasped as he covered my belly protectively. "What if it hadn't gone right? What if it had gone wrong?"

"It did go right. Stop worrying."

He kissed me on the forehead. "I can't. You're everything to me, sweetheart. When a woman holds your whole life in her hands, it's pretty damn scary," he grumbled.

Knowing I'd feel the same way if the roles were reversed and something had happened that could have meant injury to him, I'd be frantic. The way we loved, the way we needed each other *was* rather frightening. But I wouldn't want it any other way.

I loved him with every fiber of my being. And I didn't even want to think about how I'd feel if something happened to him.

"Are you happy?" I asked him.

His gray eyes met mine and held my gaze as he said, "You know I am. There's nothing in this world I want more than you, and this child we made. But I think this pregnancy is going to take years off my life."

"No, it's not. I feel great," I argued. "In fact, I've never felt better."

"I love you. I'll make sure you stay healthy," he vowed. "I need to feed you, then get you into bed."

I straddled him and then threaded my hands through his spiked hair. "I'd rather go to bed first," I purred, my voice full of anticipation.

I hadn't seen Blake in two weeks, and the last thing I cared about was food.

"Food," he barked. "And should we even be having sex?"

I did laugh this time because I couldn't stop myself. "I'm perfectly healthy. And I think my hormones are going crazy, because all I can think about is getting you naked."

His head hit the back of the sofa as he groaned. "Fuck."

"Exactly," I quipped and then lowered my mouth to his.

Blake was quick to snap out of his discomfort, his arms tightening around me, his hands moving possessively to grip my ass.

I savored the covetous hold he had on me as I thoroughly explored his mouth, reveling in the sensation of finally knowing he was mine.

As I raised my head, my hungry gaze met his, and my heart raced as I licked my lips.

"You're killing me," he complained noisily.

I pushed my hair from my face with a smile. "You feel pretty lively to me," I said playfully as I ground down on his evident erection.

"There is never a time I'm not hard when you're close to me," he told me huskily.

"I love you. And we're having a baby. A healthy pregnancy. My life couldn't be any better right now," I confided in a voice raw with emotion.

"Love you, too, baby," he answered just as candidly. "I'm happy. I just need time to get used to the fact that we're having a child. Hell, I still can't believe you're going to marry me."

I had his ring on my finger, and we'd been planning on a wedding in six months. I'd wanted to get moved permanently to Rocky Springs before we had the wedding there. "I'm going to get the Boston job wrapped up early."

"Good." He nodded. "Then you can marry me earlier."

"I wouldn't argue about that." No doubt I'd be physically showing by the time we got married, but it didn't matter to me. Having Blake Colter become my partner and husband would still be the happiest day of my life.

"I want to change my lifestyle. If we're having a baby, I don't want to be traveling all the time," he rumbled.

"We'll talk about it." Blake had to think about whether he wanted to run for re-election soon. "I don't want you to give up anything just to be with me."

"We'll compromise," he insisted. "Right now you're giving up your travel to work in-state."

"That's not a hardship," I explained for the twentieth time. "I can do plenty of jobs in Colorado. And we want to not be separated for weeks at a time."

"Then maybe I won't run for re-election."

"Or maybe you will, and I'll work my jobs around your time in DC." I was a lot more flexible than he was. And traveling back and forth with him wasn't exactly a hardship.

"We missed out on twelve years. I'm not going to miss you anymore."

I smiled at him tenderly, the yearning in his deep baritone touching me heart and soul. "We can figure it out," I promised.

He nodded. "Right after dinner," he pronounced.

"Which will be right after this." I speared my hands into his hair and swiveled my hips to encourage him to see things my way.

"Food, woman. You're pregnant," he replied in a growly voice.

"I ate lunch," I argued. "I need you more."

"I'll always need you, Harper. And I always have. You were what was missing from my life."

I sighed. "Take me to bed, Blake."

He rose slowly, letting me lock my legs around his waist. "I'll give you what you want…this time. Probably because I can't stop myself."

"All I want is you," I whispered into his ear as he carried me to the bedroom.

"You have me," he answered in a raspy voice.

"Finally," I agreed with a sigh, laying my head against his shoulder.

Maybe I hadn't always realized that I'd been waiting for this man, and this time in my life to claim him. When I hadn't known that it was Blake who had been my savior all those years ago, I'd hated myself because I thought I'd fallen for Marcus. But even then, I'd never been able to quite convince myself that I didn't need the man who'd so sweetly been my first. Little did I know that the man I needed wasn't Marcus, and I had all the reason in the world to still be in love with the guy who'd rescued me on the snowy night so long ago.

For the first time since I'd become an adult, my life finally made sense again, because the love of my life was *Blake* Colter, and always had been.

"Are you sure we should be doing this?" Blake asked uncertainly as he laid me gently on the massive bed.

Hesitation from a man usually so sure of himself humbled me. I knew it was originating from his concern for me and our baby, and his vulnerability touched my heart.

"I'm positive," I replied as I wrapped my arms around his body as he lowered himself to the bed. "If we don't, I'm going to be a very cranky pregnant woman. Hormones," I reminded him teasingly.

He grinned. "You never get crabby, but I'm sure as hell not going to risk it."

I nodded. "Smart man," I observed.

His smile was wickedly seductive as he proceeded to show me just how brilliant he could be.

~The End~

Please visit me at:
http://www.authorjsscott.com
http://www.facebook.com/authorjsscott

You can write to me at
jsscott_author@hotmail.com

You can also tweet
@AuthorJSScott

Please sign up for my Newsletter for updates, new releases and exclusive excerpts.

Books by J. S. Scott:

The Billionaire's Obsession Series:

The Billionaire's Obsession

Heart of The Billionaire

The Billionaire's Salvation

The Billionaire's Game

Billionaire Undone

Billionaire Unmasked

Billionaire Untamed

Billionaire Unbound

Billionaire Undaunted

Billionaire Unknown

Billionaire Unveiled

The Sinclairs:

The Billionaire's Christmas

No Ordinary Billionaire

The Forbidden Billionaire

The Billionaire's Touch

The Billionaire's Voice

The Billionaire Takes All

The Walker Brothers:

Release!

Player!

A Dark Horse Novel:

Bound

Hacked

The Vampire Coalition Series:

The Vampire Coalition: The Complete Collection

Ethan's Mate

Rory's Mate

Nathan's Mate

Liam's Mate

Daric's Mate

The Sentinel Demons:

The Sentinel Demons: The Complete Collection

A Dangerous Bargain

A Dangerous Hunger

A Dangerous Fury

A Dangerous Demon King

The Curve Collection: Big Girls And Bad Boys

The Changeling Encounters Collection

CPSIA information can be obtained
at www.ICGtesting.com
Printed in the USA
LVOW08s0006150317
527246LV00001B/55/P